# ANGRY Annie

a novel

DAWN L. CHILETZ

Angry Annie

Cover Design: Murphy Rae
www.murphyrae.net
Editing: Emily Lawrence
Formatting: Uplifting Designs
www.uplifting-designs.com



ISBN-13:978-1721738847
ISBN-10:1721738843

For everyone who doesn't suck.
You know who you are.

Dear Reader:

STOP. Don't waste your time going any further. This book sucks like a plunger in a toilet bowl. I don't know what to say about this woman's lack of talent. I'd like to call her an author, but just because you put a bunch of words on paper doesn't make you a writer. Heck, my cousin's five-year-old granddaughter wrote a three-sentence story about pizza that's better than this. Dawn . . . what kind of '70s hippie name is that, anyway? People name their kid Dawn when they're too lazy to think of a real name. I've always preferred dusk to Dawn and she's reminded me why. Go watch TV instead. Save your money. You're welcome.

Annie McClintonuck

# CHAPTER One

"WHO IN THE HELL is Annie McClintonuck and where does she get off?" I cringe, realizing I not only shouted but also swore loudly at work. "Hold on."

Lifting my headset off my right ear, I push off from my desk with my feet and roll my chair toward the outer edge of my cubicle. I cautiously peek around the corner to check if anyone is coming to scold me. The murmur of people on their phones and the clicking of keys on laptops is reassuring and annoyingly familiar. No one is paying attention to me as usual. I guess after two years of hearing me swear, they don't care anymore. I tend to raise my voice when I'm mad and right now I'm angry enough to chop off this Annie's head and use it for a bowling ball.

With one forceful push of my feet, I return to the desk in my gray square of hell. I reposition the headset over my ears and tuck a stray strand of my blond hair inside the earpiece. "Okay, I'm back. How dare this bimbo leave such a crappy review of your bakery? How in the fuck does she know you don't know the difference between salt and sugar? And why would she say your cookies look like they were made by a rookie? Has she ever seen one? No! No one has because you haven't opened yet!"

"Relax, Joss. It's a big deal, but not the way you're thinking," she says with a chuckle.

I don't know how she can laugh at a time like this. Why is she so calm? Her bakery opens next week and a review like this could ruin everything for her.

"It's really the best thing that could have ever happened," she says confidently.

Leaning my head on my hand, my frustration grows. Even though my little sister is only fourteen months younger than me, I swear I'm at least ten years older mentally. Jorgie doesn't get mad. She laughs and shrugs when someone is nasty. I'd call her naïve if I didn't admire her so much. She's sweet and genuine, with a heart of gold. She takes in every stray she finds and loves the shit out of everyone. Basically, she's the opposite of me.

I trust no one. My weapons are sarcasm and intimidation. I think people are trying to steal my air if they stand too close. People say I'm aggressive, but I prefer assertive. If you don't say what you want, you're never going to get it. That is, unless you're Jorgie. The world seems to come to her while I have to fight my way through everything. It's hard to believe we grew up in the same house with the same parents. As the oldest, it's not only my job to point out when she's too trusting, but also to beat the hell out of anyone who hurts her. This Annie chick did a number on her and, for some reason, Jorgie is completely underreacting to this review. It's exactly why I need to make it right.

Scrolling my mouse over Annie's words on the website, I notice there are ten comments to it. Now fifteen. Holy hell . . . thirty!

"Jorg! Thirty people . . . oh shit, thirty five people have responded to her review. This is bad. Really bad!"

"How many?" She claps her hands and howls like it's the best news she's ever heard.

"Did you forget to take your pills this morning?" I ask sarcastically. "Go on there and delete her feedback before it's too late."

"For a journalist who follows every little news blip the way you do, I can't believe you've never heard of Angry Annie!"

"First of all, I'm a wannabe journalist. Researching other people's information just makes me a paid stalker. Secondly, her nickname is Angry Annie?" I huff. "That's fitting. She seems like a nasty little bitch." Reaching into my desk drawer, I open a bottle of ibuprofen and pop two into my mouth. I'm getting a stress headache.

"That's what people call her around here. From what I've heard, she lives outside the city limits and has made a name for herself by leaving bad reviews for everything she comes across. Go look her up on Amazon. She's left well over two hundred. They're hysterical. The millennials think she rocks."

I roll my eyes at her. I've always hated being called a millennial. Just because I'm only twenty-five doesn't mean I don't care about things. It's ridiculous to be lumped into a group because I was born in a certain decade. I can't believe she thinks it's some kind of honor.

"I'm more concerned about your business than Amazon's. You've worked really hard. Plus, you have your life savings invested in this. It can't afford this type of negative publicity."

"Mm . . . negative. Uh-huh."

"Dammit, Jorgina! You need to listen to me. I think we should take out more ad space in the neighborhood *Patch.* Maybe even retort her claims."

"Ooh, we're using formal names? Okay, Joslyn, are you still on my website?"

"Yeah." I'm certain she can sense my irritation by the way I elongate the word.

"Read some of the comments."

Scrolling my mouse over the page, I choose a random response. "If Angry Annie says this place sucks, then I'm definitely going there opening day. Bring your cash, people! If she says it's bad, it's probably fantastic!"

I move to another. "I can't wait to see if Annie's right or wrong. I follow all her reviews and I always have to check it out for myself!"

Each comment contains positive responses to Annie's negative ones. I lean forward in my chair, awestruck.

"I can only assume you're eating crow because you're quiet," she says with a smile.

I can tell she's smiling because I know how her words sound when she's gloating.

"What kind of sorcery is this?" I mumble.

"I wish I knew her. I bet she's a riot."

"Hmm . . ." My brain suddenly goes into overdrive as I'm struck with a brilliant idea. "I gotta go, Jorg.

We'll talk later."

She starts to say something as I end the call. I'm on a mission and when I'm focused, I can't talk at the same time I'm trying to think. My fingers dance over the keys and I snarl. "I'm coming for you, Angry Annie."

# CHAPTER Two

MY LEG THUMPS LIKE a rabbit as I watch Darla scan my article submission. When I found out Darla Fender was the managing editor of *The Gaggle,* I knew I had to get a job with her. She's won an Ellie award for her editorials and is extremely well known across the globe for her innovations in journalism and willingness to take risks. I keep hoping someday she'll take one of those risks on me. Especially today.

I took a job as a mailroom clerk at the magazine right out of college and have worked my way up to a fact-checker, which basically means I spend all day making sure other people's thoughts are accurate.

I've submitted an article idea almost every week since I started. At first, she gawked when I had the nerve to approach her, then she got annoyed. Eventually, she learned that if she took the paper directly from my hand, I wouldn't keep asking her if she got it. Now, she usually skims it and says she'll get back to me. But *this* time she's actually reading it in front of me. I'm about to toss my lunch.

She places the paper on her desk and slides her reading glasses down to the tip of her nose. "Okay, Joslyn. You have my attention. Explain yourself."

I clear my throat and pinch my leg to steady my nerves.

"Trolls are a source of disdain across the Internet. They are a group of narcissists, sadists, and masochists who take pleasure from inflicting pain on others, usually in the form of reviews for products and services. Another term for this is Schadenfreude, which means someone who gets joy from other people's failures and humiliation. They use harassment and exaggeration to wreak havoc on businesses, novels, online merchandise . . . anything where they can hurt someone else. I've recently learned that one such troll lives in our community. Not only is she well-known on social media, but she has a following."

I wipe the sweat from my palms on my skirt as Darla sighs. God, I hope I'm not boring her. *Get to the point, Joss.*

"My proposal is that I get close to this troll, learn all about her life and expose her to the world. We would make an example out of her and bring the truth about these savages to light. The world wants to know what makes someone with no soul find pleasure in creating drama for complete strangers. They need to stop."

She taps her fingers on her desk and stares at me for what seems like an eternity. She turns to her laptop and moves the mouse around on the screen. "You're cur*rently working as a fact-checker for Claus, correct?"*

"Yes."

"Do you not enjoy your position here?"

I know my mouth is gaping, but I can't help it. My nerves slip away and my fighting nature pushes to the surface.

"Of course I do. I love my job, but my goal has always been to be a journalist. All I want is an opportunity to prove to you I can write a gripping story that will draw in readers. Knowing you started off as a courier for a newspaper, I'd hoped you would appreciate my desire to better myself and my position."

Did her lip curl or am I imagining it?

She leans back in her chair and studies me briefly before she stands and walks around her desk. Leaning on the corner, her eyes move from my head to my toes and back up again. She crosses her arms and stares at me. I'm not sure if she's trying to intimidate me or not, but I'm the queen of stare downs. I will not buckle even though the fact I'm in the same room as her and she knows my name makes me slightly giddy.

After a few minutes, I realize she's never going to cave. I'm in the presence of a Jedi master. I'm not worthy. Should I let her win? What do I do?

"So?" I ask, angry with myself for giving in but knowing it was the right thing to do.

She shrugs and walks back to her chair. "It has promise, but you have a job here and it's not writing articles. If you want to pass your idea on to Claus, you can see if he's willing to do the legwork. Good day, Ms. Walters."

She sits down in her chair and begins typing on her computer. Did I just get the brush off? I was so close. What did I do wrong? My legs are frozen. I can't move. I refuse to move. No. This can't be over.

"But, it's my idea. I don't want to give it to Claus. I want to write it myself."

She continues to type, ignoring me. Am I wearing the cloak of invisibility? I bite my lip. I need to think quickly.

"What if I write it on my own time? It won't interfere with my work and if I have to, I'll take all my personal time to get it done. You can read what I've written and if you hate it, I promise to not bother you again for . . . say . . . three months?"

Her eyes suddenly shift to me. "Three months?" She almost seems happy.

Am I that bad? My heart drops knowing she wants time away from me. I'm certain everyone I work with thinks I'm a pain in the ass. I guess I can add her name to the list. "Yes. Three months. I promise."

She removes her glasses and folds her fingers. Her brows furrow as she speaks. "If you do it on your own time and it does not interfere with your work, then I'll consider it. However, I'm making no promises to you that anything will happen with it. Even if on the off chance it's decent, it doesn't mean it will get published. You can't simply talk about her. You need to find out why she writes the reviews. You'll need at least three to four examples, with facts, and will have to define her thought process. I will expect you to remain professional at all times while representing the magazine. We'll need a signed release. You'll need to consult the legal department for any possibility of slander, and you will keep your mouth shut about this discussion. The last thing I need is twenty more Joslyns chasing me around the office thinking if they bother me enough,

I'll give them a shot. Do you understand?"

She might have just insulted me, but I don't care. I nod excitedly and immediately hustle my way to the door before she changes her mind.

"And, Joslyn . . . I'm going to hold you to those three months."

"Thank you. Once you've read my work, I'm confident it'll be you looking for me next time."

She starts typing again and dismisses me with her hand. At this point, there's nothing anyone could say or do to bring me down from this high. Angry Annie just became my favorite person in the world. Now I just have to find her.

# CHAPTER Three

WHEN I SAID I was a professional stalker, I wasn't kidding. I once found a guy's full name, address, and social media profile off a picture on Tinder. Before I met him for coffee, I knew his parents' names, where he and his best friend went on vacation, and his favorite ice cream flavor. I often wonder if my knack for research is one of the reasons I'm extremely single. But honestly, I don't really care much for dating. It's a lot of fake smiles and pretending to be interested in stuff you find boring. I already do that half the day at work. I don't need it in my personal life too. Lately, every guy I've met is just blah and ho-hum. Plus, I'm a career driven woman and men slow you down. Sometimes I have to remind my hoo-ha of that when she's screaming for attention. But we all have to make sacrifices, even my girly parts.

Despite my superb investigative skills, this Annie chick has evaded me. How can someone have an Amazon account but zero social presence? She doesn't have an Instagram, Facebook, or Twitter account under her real name or nickname. There's no LinkedIn account and she's not listed in the white pages. I can find numerous mentions of Angry Annie all over the Internet along with local reviews she's left, but no one has ever seen her or knows her personally. I'm starting to think she's catfishing and maybe she's not really a "she" after all. My dreams begin to slip away like butter off corn on the cob until I remember Adam Donovan. I sit up a little straighter in my chair and check the time on my cell phone. It's almost six o'clock on a Friday night. That means that if he's still a creature of habit, by seven he'll be off work and headed to Tyke's Tavern for a beer.

I met Adam on a blind date about three years ago. For some reason, my sister thought a cop would make a good match for me. He's a nice guy and all, and I could tell he really liked me, but he was too eager. He started asking me how many kids I wanted within the first hour. I could tell he was the kind of guy who thought men should work and women should take care of the children. I was done with him when he asked if I knew how to cook. But, I know he's still single because we're Facebook friends. I truly believe in keeping all your bridges intact and never burning them. You never know when you'll need someone. Tonight, I need Adam Donovan.

I usually stay at work until 8:00 myself, but I've already finished all my research for Claus and wrote up all my reports for him even though they aren't due until next week. Half the staff is here, as usual. We're all workaholics, but I don't think anyone will care if I slip out.

As I walk toward the elevator, I notice Darla is still

working and in a meeting with two ad execs. Her office is made of glass and completely visible to the staff. She says she has nothing to hide and I believe her. She's above reproach, tough as nails, and a shrewd leader who demands excellence from everyone she encounters. She's everything I hope to be someday. I watch her move about the room and try to read her lips. What I wouldn't give to shadow her for a day. I could learn so much. I smile as I picture myself at her desk in a designer suit and Christian Louboutin heels. Someday, I'll have her job. I make that promise to myself every day before I leave work. It's reaffirming and keeps me working toward the prize when I'm tired.

After a tense thirty-minute drive, I finally arrive. It's a Friday night, so I expect Tyke's to be crowded, but this is ridiculous. I scan the room for Adam and a wave of relief settles my nerves when I spot him playing pool in the back corner.

I move to the bar to check my reflection in a small corner of the mirror and unbutton two buttons of my blouse. I fluff my long blond hair and run my fingers through the ends to make sure it looks sexy, but not like I tried. I need to use every weapon in my arsenal to get what I want from him. As I pull down on my shirt to straighten it, I confirm in my mind that tonight's weapon is my cleavage.

I catch a faraway glimpse of a stranger in the reflection of the mirror. His bright white teeth stand out along his dark, scruffy beard. He immediately draws my attention. He appears to be smiling at me. He shakes his head and lifts his beer to his lips, never losing eye contact. I strain to watch him in the mirror as a crowd moves behind me, blocking my view. Turning around, I look for him over and around heads, but he's gone. It's as if he was never there to begin with although I'm certain I still feel his eyes on me. He was quite alluring.

"What's a nice girl like you doing in a place like this?"

I turn toward the familiar voice. The prey has sought out the predator. "Well, hello there, Adam. Can't a girl grab a beer after a long day of work?" I flip my hair and tilt my head to the side before smiling at him like he's a home-cooked meal and I'm starving. The responding look on his face tells me he's already planning our children's names in his head.

"You can have anything you want when I'm around." He snaps his fingers in the air to get the bartender's attention. He's pouring a whiskey and makes direct eye contact with Adam's fingers right before he turns to help someone else. I try not to snicker at Adam's audacity. He should know that type of behavior is a surefire way to get spit in your drink. Just because he's a cop doesn't mean he owns the joint. Respect goes a long way with everyone.

"No, no," I begin. "You're not paying for my drink. I don't want you thinking I owe you something at the end of the night." I wink as I grab ahold of his arm and lean toward him.

He's speechless and I know I have him right where I want him. I rest my forearms on the bar, smile, and am immediately served. Adam tries to pay, but the bartender takes the cash from my hand, ignoring him. With a cold one in my hand, Adam and I walk toward a booth in the back corner. When I slide into the seat, he slides in next to me instead of across from me. No surprise.

I know I'm laying it on thick to get his attention, but damn, he's way too close. I'm getting tired and bored. I need to get this over with.

"You know, sometimes I wish I'd gone into law enforcement."

"You? You're too pretty to be a cop."

"That's so sweet of you to say." I touch his arm and let my fingers linger for a moment. "But, if I were a police officer, then I'd get to work with you."

"That's very true, but you don't need to work with me to see me. You could see me every night if you wanted to."

"Oh, I wish. I never seem to have the time for stuff like that." I sigh heavily. "Work, work, work. It's all I do. I've got this big project and I'm really struggling." I bat my eyes and force them to water, hoping to play on his emotions. I sniff and turn away from him.

"Hey . . . Are you okay? What's going on?"

"I don't want to bother you with all my problems."

"You're not bothering me. It's my job to be a good listener and you know I'd do anything for you."

"You would?" I bring a napkin to my eyes.

Adam scoots in a little closer. "Tell me what's got you so upset."

"Well . . . my boss has me doing this research project and I'm supposed to find this lady who has some facts we need to confirm a story. I've done everything I can think of and I don't know how to contact her. If I don't get a quote from her, I think he's going to fire me. I really wish I had her address."

His brows furrow immediately. I can tell he's worried about crossing a line.

I place my hand on his thigh. "But like I said, it's my problem. Let's talk about something else." I suck in a few breaths like I'm fighting back tears.

He places his hand on mine. "I wish I could help you, but I'm not supposed to use my records access for personal stuff."

"I know. I didn't want to talk about it. Forget it. You know, I think I should go. Could you let me out?"

I grab my purse and motion for him to move.

"You don't have to go already, do you?"

He's staring at me so earnestly, I almost feel bad. Ugh. Why did I think this would work? I ponder the idea of coming clean but then decide to forget my dumb plan to lure him into helping me. I'll figure out how to find Annie another way.

"Adam, I'm sorry. Just forget I said anything. Really. I do need to go."

He moves and as I stand, he stares down at the ground, concerned. I place a soft kiss on his cheek. It's the least I can do for being such a flirt.

"It was good to see you. Take care."

I turn toward the exit and he grabs my arm.

"I suppose I could do it this once. But you can't tell anyone."

My eyes bulge as my heart skips in my chest. "Are you sure? I don't want you to get into trouble."

"Ah, I won't. It's not like I've never looked up an address of a girl I liked before. What's the difference?"

I secretly wonder if he's referring to me. The idea that he knows where I live slightly concerns me, but he seems harmless. I smile in response and pull a small notebook from my purse along with a pen. "Her name is Annie McClintonuck. I don't know anything about her other than that she lives around here. But how many McClintonucks can there be?" I laugh and he grins.

I write down her name and hand it to him. He reaches for the paper but places his hand over mine instead.

"I'll do it on one condition."

"Okay. What?" I'm almost afraid to know.

"You have to let me take you on a real date. Just the two of us. No sister. And not to a bar."

"But, it's so late."

"Not tonight. When you're less stressed. Maybe next week?"

Ugh. I stare down at the paper and wonder if a night with Adam is worth Annie's address. In my mind I see the byline of my article on the front page of *The Gaggle* and I know what I have to do.

"You got yourself a date."

# CHAPTER Four

AS I GLANCE THROUGH my passenger window at Annie's house, I check and recheck the address to make sure it matches the info from Adam. The small, orange, brick ranch is in an older neighborhood within walking distance of town. I love the mature trees up and down the street. They almost make it feel like I'm in the country. The yard is impeccably groomed. The grass is lush and dark green even with the drought we've had this summer. The bushes have been trimmed with the precision of a surgeon and gorgeous flowers line the walkway to the door. I'd think Anne of Green Gables lived here if not for the bars on the windows and garbage piled by the front door.

I'd contemplated following her and purposely running into her somewhere to befriend her, but I've been watching her house for the last two hours and there's been no movement. My fingers drum on the leather-wrapped steering wheel. I don't have a lot of time to write this article, and who knows how long it would take to make friends with someone like her.

It's possible she isn't home, but it's 9:00 a.m. on a Saturday morning. Unless she's up and at 'em early, chances are she's still in there. She's probably on her computer trying to find another person's life to ruin.

"Plan B," I say out loud to no one as I grab my bag and open the car door. I stroll up the walkway to her front door with absolutely no idea what I'm going to say to her. But I'm good under pressure, so I'm certain I'll think of something.

The black bars on the windows and door make me wonder if there's a lot of crime in the neighborhood. Glancing behind me and then at both neighbors' houses, I notice they don't have bars. Strange. Is she paranoid or are they careless?

There are two dirty plates and a Tupperware container by her front door along with a garbage bag that seems to have a comforter in it. I swat away the flies. Gross.

Lifting my hand to ring the bell, a piece of paper near the door catches my eye. I squat slightly to read it.

"No solicitors. I don't like cookies. I've found my Lord and Savior. I already have an alarm. I don't need you to cut my grass. I don't like raffle tickets or children. I don't care if you're putting yourself through school, I'm not buying. I don't donate anything to anyone. Beware the dog, he bites. I don't need any new friends. I don't care if you just moved in. I know who I'm voting for and don't want to hear your opinions. Don't ring the bell. Don't knock. Don't stand on my porch. Go away!"

Wow. She's a real peach. I pull the paper off the door and stuff it into my bag. Then, I ring the bell. A loud barking dog responds to the push of the button and takes me aback. I expect it to continue for a while, but it stops barking after a few seconds. No one comes to the door, so I ring it again. The dog starts barking then stops, like before. I have a theory, so I ring the bell three times in a row and the barking stops and stutters. Her door chime is a dog. Okay . . . I knock on the door. No barking this time. Her sign should warn to beware the dog *chime* not the dog.

I stand and wait and still, no one answers. There's a small window panel alongside the door, so I cup my hands around my face and glance inside. I can't see much, and I press my face into the bars to get a better view.

I can make out a hall that leads to what seems to be the kitchen. Just as I'm trying to focus on the furniture, someone steps in front of the window and I shriek, stumbling back.

The door opens forcibly and the bars are the only thing between me and the small old woman standing in front of me.

"Can't you read?" she shouts.

I cough and place my hand on my heart to steady myself.

"Do-you-know-En-glish?" she asks, enunciating every syllable slowly.

"Hi, I'm so sorry to bother you, but I was looking for Annie McClintonuck. Do you know her?"

Her hands fly to her hips. "What part of 'don't knock' do you not understand?"

"What do you mean?" I ask, feigning innocence.

"The sign, woman! Read the sign!"

She starts to close the door and I shout, "What sign?"

She huffs and points to the outside of the door. I shrug and shake my head.

"Oh, for the love of all things holy." She mumbles the words as she unlocks the bars, reaches her hand around the door, and feels for the paper that isn't there.

I pull my bag tightly against my waist.

"Well, son of a nutcracker's ass. If that boy took my sign, I'll beat him with my broom."

She's loud and fierce for a tiny little thing. I'm convinced by her stance she could take me if she wanted to. She looks strong. I wonder if Annie moved. What if this isn't her address after all?

I clear my throat. "Anyway, I was wondering if you could tell me where I could find Annie McClintonuck."

"What you want with her? She owe you money?"

I fake a small laugh. "Oh, gosh no. I was actually hoping I could give her some."

Where did that come from? I don't have money to give away.

"Hmm . . . Give her money? She win the lottery?"

Money drives the world. She seems a little more interested in talking, so I go with it. "No, but there's some cash waiting for her if she's willing to speak to me." I cautiously peer over her head to see if anyone else is inside.

"You lose something?" she asks. "Ain't nothin' in my house for you to see."

"Oh, so you do live here." My shoulders slump. I guess this is the wrong address after all. "Do you have any idea where I can find Annie?"

The intensity with which she stares at me makes me straighten up. She's silent as she crosses her arms. I hear a clicking noise that seems to be coming from her mouth even though I don't see it moving. Is this another stare down match? Here I go again. Why does everyone insist on starting a contest with me lately?

"Could you answer the question?" I don't have time for games. I have an article to write.

"How much money?" she asks. "And whatchoo need her to tell you?"

"I really need to have this conversation with Annie. If you could just tell me where I can find her then I can—"

"You lookin' at her. How much money?"

"You're Annie?" I say with a chuckle. She's got to be kidding me.

"Are you slow or something? You got medical issues? I swear. Just my luck someone comes knockin' with money and it's gotta be a dopey damsel with no fashion sense. You get those shoes from Walmart? Or did you steal them off a homeless person?"

What a bitch! Holy crap, maybe this is her after all. "Annie?" I question. "Annie McClintonuck?"

"Oh, for the sake of fuck, did I stutter?"

"Hi, umm . . . Annie, my name is Joslyn Walters. I'm relieved to have finally found you."

"Child, you better not be wasting my time. You said you had money. Now tell me how much or get off my stoop and go climb back into that heap you drive. I got stuff to do. I don't care who you are and I don't wanna hear none of your pleasantries. Spit out what you gotta say or move on."

Angry Annie is *really* angry. And she's old. Her hair is dark in places, but the gray is more apparent. So are all the wrinkles around her eyes. I'd say she had laugh lines around her mouth if I thought she knew how to smile. My guess is they're from years of frowning at people. I don't know why I imagined her to be a big-titted bimbo. I gaze at her chest. Well, maybe she still is. At this point, anything is possible. She wants straightforward, so I give it to her.

"I'm a reporter for *The Gaggle.*"

"The gurgle?"

"Gaggle. The magazine?" There's zero recognition on her face. She must not have left one of her nasty reviews for them, yet. "Anyway, we're doing a piece about people who leave online reviews. You have quite a following online and our readers would love to know more about you and how you go about testing products."

She rolls her eyes. "I still haven't heard any mention of dollar bills."

Shit. She's going to want that money. Darla didn't give me a budget. As a matter of fact, I'm certain there would never be one. Should I offer to pay her out of my own pocket? How much money is in my checkbook right now? I answer as if there isn't an issue.

"Of course we'd be willing to pay you for your time." I'm such a good liar.

"How much?"

"One hundred dollars?" Shit. I shouldn't have posed that as a question.

Her eyes squint and she waves me off as she turns to reenter the house.

"I mean today. Just for today."

She turns. "How many days?"

I ponder the question. What do I need to know and how long will it take? "Well, that depends on what you're willing to share. The more you give me, the more I pay."

"I'm listening."

"I want to know what made you start leaving reviews. What motivates you? How do you pick the items or places? Why do you do what you do?"

Annie swats at a fly. "These damn bugs. I don't like being out here."

"Let's go inside then."

"Well, damn. I guess my memory has flown the coop 'cause I don't remember ever inviting you anywhere."

She's a tough cookie. I decide on reverse psychology. "Look, I have an article to write. If you're not interested in the money, I have a list of other reviewers I can contact who would be more than willing to tell me their stories."

I spin on my heel and hop down her stairs. Concern washes over me. I offer a silent prayer that Annie needs money as much as I think she does. As my hand reaches for the door handle of my car, she finally speaks.

"I won't talk for less than five hundred."

I'm relieved to hear her voice and exasperated at the same time. "Five hundred? That's a lot of money. Why would I pay you that much?"

"'Cause I'm famous. 'Cause I got stuff to say that people wanna hear. You said it yourself. Now you can go talk to those other folks you got on your list, but I can guarantee there isn't anyone on it half as interesting as me."

Annie's arms swirl around her head. "These flies are Satan's spawn."

I point toward her front door. "If you didn't leave your dirty dishes on the porch, then maybe you wouldn't have flies."

"They ain't my dishes."

What the hell? "Whose dishes are they?"

"I ain't telling you nothin' else till I see some green."

I put on my best poker face while I calculate whether or not I can afford to give this woman five hundred dollars for a story. What if she's boring? What if I can't get enough out of her to expose her? I need to know how she operates and something tells me, she's going to be hard to crack. This is going to take some time. I'm going to have to follow her if I want to know things. Maybe I should take some vacation time. Is it even worth it?

I scratch my head. If I write this story and impress Darla, maybe she'll give me other assignments. I'll be a journalist before I know it and I'll be glad I spent the money. Maybe I should think of it as an investment. I wonder if I can deduct it on my taxes. Chewing on the inside of my cheek for a moment, I make a decision.

"I'll tell you what," I begin. "I'll give you a check for fifty dollars today and another for four hundred and fifty at the end of the week, assuming you make it worth my while."

"A check? Do I look like a bank? Girl . . . in my world, checks bounce higher than a man's balls during sex. I want cash or no deal."

I sigh. Nothing here is going to be easy. I can feel it. "How about this . . . I'll give you twenty bucks today to talk to me for an hour. Then you have nothing to lose. I'll get you your cash and pay you daily to let me follow you around."

"Nu-uh. You ain't hanging around me all day long. I got things to do."

"Like what? Do you need to leave more reviews for products you've never tried?"

She crosses her arms and marches down her stairs toward me. I realize I'm a little scared of her, but I don't want her to notice, so I hold my ground.

"Who says I haven't tried stuff? Who? You tell me!"

I open my mouth with the full intention of calling her out on my sister's bakery review, but I stop myself. "Prove it then. Show me."

Annie glances up at the sun and places her palm over her eyes to see me better. I can hear her grinding her teeth.

"Tick tock, Annie."

"Fine. Give me the twenty." She holds out her hand.

I reach into my purse and pull out the cash. She holds the bill up to the light, flicks it twice, then turns and walks back into the house.

Where is she going? I stand next to my car, unsure what I'm supposed to do. Did she just take the money and run?

After a few minutes and no word from Annie, I walk up to her door. I stand there for a few minutes, listening to see if she's coming back. The sound of a lawnmower next door makes me twist my head, but I don't see anyone.

"If you're waiting for a written invitation to come in, then you're gonna be standing out there until pigs fly," she shouts from inside.

The door squeaks as I open it. Once I'm inside, the smell of bread makes my mouth immediately water. Her house is surprisingly charming. I'm not sure what I expected, but this wasn't it. I think I half-expected to see the hearts of her victims mounted on the walls like trophies and outlines of people she's murdered on the carpet. But it's tidy and organized. Her furniture seems like it could be antique. There's an old wood smell mixed with the bread that almost makes me think of my late grandmother.

"Hey, Stupid!" she yells. "If you want to eat breakfast, you have two minutes to get your ugly little ass in here or it's going in the garbage."

Jeez, she's nasty. I swear if I didn't know I was going to expose her for the fraud she is, I might be inclined to tell her to go fuck herself. She has no right to talk to me that way. I hustle my way to the kitchen to set her straight about how she addresses me, but before I get there, my stomach growls. I decide I'll correct her right after I eat whatever smells so divine.

She has her back to me while she washes dishes in the sink, but I notice she's set a small bowl out for me at the kitchen table. I slide into the picnic bench style seat and bend down to sniff it. It smells and looks hideous. Do I suffer and eat it or risk offending her by turning it away? Ugh. She didn't even leave me a fork.

"Do you have some type of utensil for me?" I ask

hesitantly.

She pivots to regard me and the bowl in my hand. Her eyes start to dance with amusement. Before I know it, she's laughing hysterically and slapping her legs with her palms as she hops about the room from foot to foot.

I'm not sure why she thinks I'm so damn funny and to be honest, she's really pissing me off.

"You know what? You have no business calling me stupid or any other name. I'll have you know I graduated at the top of my class, with honors."

Her laughter intensifies.

"I don't appreciate your attitude or the venom you spew. If you expect me to eat . . . whatever this is, then the least you could do is set out silverware of some kind."

Annie grabs ahold of the counter and gasps for breaths as she laughs. She gets to a point where she's heaving and there's no longer sound. As upset as I am with her, she almost makes me want to laugh too. I start off with a small smile, then a giggle. I don't know what I said that was so funny, but I make Jorgie laugh all the time. Maybe I don't even realize my own talent.

After a few minutes, she pulls a kitchen towel to her eyes to dry the tears that have formed. "Ooh, child . . . I haven't laughed that hard in years."

I shrug. "I'm glad I'm so entertaining." I swirl the bowl around in my hands and bring it up to sniff it one more time. "What do you call this dish?"

"Around here I call it cat food."

"What?" I place the bowl down on the table. "You were going to serve me cat food?"

"I wasn't planning on serving you anything. But if you're that hungry, I suppose you can have it."

"You told me to get my ass in here and eat," I reply.

She leans her hand on the counter and swirls her tongue around her teeth, making that annoying clicking sound I heard earlier. "I thought you said your name was Joslyn."

"It is."

"Do you usually respond to Stupid? That some kind of nickname maybe your momma gave you?"

I feel a headache starting. I take a deep breath so I don't explode. "No, I don't answer to stupid, and I think it was rude of you to call me that."

A small meow sounds from the doorway. A yellow tabby cat prances into the room.

"You're late," Annie says. "That woman almost ate your breakfast." She stuffs the towel into her pocket and motions from me to the cat. "Stupid the woman, meet Stupid the cat. I didn't know anyone could be dumber than him."

My mouth drops and I close my eyes. What in the world have I gotten myself into?

# CHAPTER Five

"HIS NAME IS STUPID?" I ask as his tail swirls around my hand. At least someone in this house is friendly.

"He showed up one day. I opened the front door to get my paper and he ran in. I gave up trying to get him to leave. He's as dumb as a doornail. He walks into things all the time."

"Maybe he can't see well." I bend down to lift him onto my lap.

The sound of the lawnmower outside gets louder. Annie and I both glance out her back window at the same time. There's a broad-shouldered man with his back to us, cutting her grass. He's wearing a baseball cap, no shirt, and jeans. Yowza.

"That damn boy is always getting in my way." She opens the back door of the house and yells, "How many times do I have to tell you I don't want you cuttin' my grass? You hard of hearin'?"

The lawnmower stops and he turns around. Holy mother of mercy he's gorgeous. If I had a lawn, I'd hire him to mow mine. My girly lawn wonders if he's skilled in that area as well.

He waves his hand and smiles. Familiar white teeth catch me off guard.

"Morning, Annie! It's a beautiful day, isn't it? How was dinner last night? Did you like my pot roast?"

"You used too much salt and it was overcooked. Your dishes are bringing flies. Either you start pickin' them up or I'm gonna throw them in the trash!"

"Sorry, Annie. I'll go grab them right now. Did you like the blanket I found for you?"

I'm certain my mouth is hanging open and I'm drooling.

"I don't need no ugly blanket. I don't know why you thought I did. I put it in a garbage bag where it belongs. Boy, you have horrible taste. It was scratchy and smelled funny."

"Darn. Well, sorry, Annie. I just saw it at the store and I thought of you. I'll go grab it and the dishes before I finish."

"I'm tryin' to have a conversation in here and your mowin' is too damn loud. Go mow someone else's lawn."

"Aww, Annie, you know I only love you like that. I'll finish it later after your guest leaves. Have a good day! Oh, how does pizza sound for dinner?" he yells back.

"If you're gonna burn the bottom and put that damn pineapple on it again then don't bother. Pineapple is a fruit. You see anybody putting strawberries on pizza? The only thing pineapple belongs in are piña coladas. You want to make me happy? Bring me one of those."

"No problem, Annie. No pineapple!" He waves to

her and smiles brightly. He lifts his cap slightly as his eyes travel to the window. I'm not sure he can see me even though my rear end is off the seat to get a better look. He tips his hat to me and smiles. My butt falls quickly back in the seat and I turn my head so I don't look like I was staring even though I totally was.

Annie slams the back door and mumbles something inaudible. She rolls her watch around her wrist and pulls it farther away as she tilts her head back, I assume to see the time. Looks like Stupid may not be the only one with vision problems.

"Counting the time you wasted already on my porch, you got thirty-five more minutes or else you're gonna have to give me another twenty."

"Who was that?" I ask, pointing toward the back yard. I place Stupid on the floor and he hops toward the doorway. He rams his head into the wall, stops, moves over a bit, and hops down the hall as if nothing happened.

"The boy? He lives next door. You wanna talk about my reviews or are we going to make chit chat all day?"

"He's a boy? He looks all man to me."

"Boy, man, they're all the same. He's annoying and won't leave me alone. He has issues."

"Really? You mean like, he's slow?"

"He's slow at everything and he doesn't listen. He's always bugging me. I wish he'd move."

"How long have you two been friends?"

"I ain't nobody's friend. Why you so interested in my neighbors? You writing an article about who lives near Annie or you writing about Annie?"

"Right. Of course, I was just curious." I brush my hair away from my face and she studies me.

"You single? You tryin' to find you a hot piece of ass?"

My face warms with a blush. "No! I mean, yes. I'm single but no, I'm not trying to find anything. I'm very focused on my career."

She motions to my waist as she leans on her kitchen counter. "If you don't use that thing regularly, it stops working, you know?"

"What thing?"

"Your kitty. You gotta keep it lubed up regularly or else it'll dry out."

I cough. This just got really uncomfortable.

"It's a fact of life, child. Every pussy needs petting."

"Um, anyway, let's talk about you."

"You wanna know about my pussy?"

"God, no. What I mean is let's discuss your online presence."

She walks out of the kitchen without saying a word.

"Did I offend you?" I holler after her.

When she doesn't respond, I get up and follow her. I glance around as I trail down the hall. There are two bedrooms I hadn't noticed. One must be where she sleeps because there's a small bed. The other has a desk with a very old cream-colored computer on it. She pushes a button and waits, tapping her foot. There's a loud whirring sound. I assume the old thing takes a while to get going.

"Is *that* what you use?" I point to the fossil in front of her.

She glances between me and her computer. "Yeah, you got a problem with that?"

"It's really old."

"Just because something is old doesn't mean it doesn't work. Old doesn't mean bad. You young people think 'cause somethin' isn't brand-new it isn't good. Sometimes older things are better."

"How old are you?" I ask.

"None of your business."

"I'm paying you to tell me about yourself, remember?" I lean my head on the doorframe and cross one foot over my ankle.

She repositions her rear end on the hardwood chair where she's sitting. "I've been seventeen four times," she says without looking at me. "You need a calculator?"

"No, I don't. Just because something isn't a dinosaur doesn't mean it's dumb."

The screen finally purrs to life. It stays blue for a long time and chugs along slowly. Jeez. I couldn't handle waiting if that were my computer. I like to get right to it.

After watching nothing happen on her computer for what seems like forever, I step into the room and over to a black and white picture on the wall. There's an attractive young woman with her arm intertwined with a handsome young man. They seem really happy. "Who's that?"

"Ain't nobody. Mind your own beeswax. I think we need to be done. I don't like you. You're nosy."

"Annie, we had a deal. I still have twenty more minutes. Plus, I'll be back tomorrow."

"Nu-uh. Tomorrow is church and I ain't bringin' your skinny, twiggy, boring ass to church with me."

"You think I'm skinny?" I choose to ignore everything after that.

She rolls her eyes, untangles the mouse cord, clicking on Word for Windows. At least she has software. I wonder if she's going to show me a review she wrote. I decide not to hover. She already wants me to leave and I haven't seen anything newsworthy yet.

"Fine, Sunday is off, but I'll be back first thing Monday morning. I think."

"You think? What's that mean? You don't know what you doin'? You ain't made a decision?"

"I just need to ask, I mean, tell work."

"Ask, tell . . . You don't fool me, missy. They know you here or you playin' them too? I bet nobody would know a thing if you went missin'."

I swallow hard. Missing? Is she planning on killing me in the basement? "They know exactly where I am. I just didn't realize this was going to take so long and I need to let them know."

"Um hmm."

She clicks on a document and it starts to print. Holy hell. Her printer is slow too. I guess she doesn't have the money for new stuff. I get a little excited when it finishes and she reads it over. I wonder if I get to see it.

She stands and leaves the room. I follow her because I'm starting to realize she's never going to tell me where she's going or come back. She walks to the kitchen, rummages through a drawer, pulls something out of it, and starts to work on the paper. I lick my lips with anticipation. This could be a copy of one of her reviews or maybe it's a new one she's been working on.

She turns to me and holds out the paper. I quickly skim it. "No solicitors. I don't like cookies. I've found my Lord and Savior. I already have an alarm. I don't need you to cut my grass . . ."

"This is the sign from your front door," I say. "Why are you giving this to me?"

"So you can put it back up where it was when you took it. On your way out."

She walks to the front door and holds it open. She rolls her tongue again and makes that damn clicking noise.

"I didn't take your sign," I respond.

"Then how'd you know what it said?"

Damn. She caught me. I walk out the door and turn to face her. "See you Monday morn—" I don't even finish my sentence when she slams the door and I hear the lock click.

I close my eyes and take a deep breath. "Great job, Joss. That went really well. You think? You think maybe you could have handled it a little better? Maybe you should have kept your mouth shut about the stupid sign." I place the paper back on the house, making sure the duct tape sticks to the brick. I sigh and turn around to face my car and that's when I see the shirtless hottie watching me. He's on his knees by Annie's flowers, picking weeds. Great.

"Do you always talk to yourself and answer?" he asks with a crooked smile. His head tilts to the side and he squints his eyes in the sun. Damn. He's even more attractive up close.

"As a matter of fact I do." I hold out my hand to him. "Joslyn Walters. I'm a writer with The Gaggle."

He stands and brushes off his hands on his stone washed jeans. My eyes linger a bit on his thighs. He reaches out and shakes my hand. "Rhode Bennett, next door neighbor."

His hands are rough. He must do a lot of manual labor. "It's nice to meet you."

"Oh, we've sort of met before," he replies.

"We have? When?"

"Our eyes met at Tyke's last night."

"That *was* you?" I reply with a smile. "I thought I recognized the teeth, although you're clean-shaven today."

He snickers as his hand washes over his chin. "Yeah, it was getting a little scraggly."

"No, it wasn't. It was hot."

His head tilts to the side and he smiles shyly.

"Shit. Did I say that out loud?"

He glances down at the dirt and his cheeks almost seem to blush. It's endearing as fuck.

"Anyway. I have to go. Nice to meet you." I shake my head at myself as I walk to my car. I glance over my shoulder and see he's watching me, so I make sure I swivel my ass a bit more.

Once I reach the car I notice him bend down to continue his work. He's not staring and it bothers me. "You think maybe I could ask you a few questions sometime?" I shout. "I'm doing a piece on Annie and I'd love to hear some stories."

"Sure," he replies. "She's a great lady. I'd be happy to tell you what I know."

"Great!" I pull a piece of paper from my notebook and scribble my cell number. "Here's my number. I, uh, ran out of business cards."

He walks over to me and takes the paper from my hands, tucking it in the back pocket of his jeans. "Thanks. I'll call you sometime."

Why does that feel like a brush-off? An even better question is why do I care if it is? On the drive home I make a decision. I'm about to put my research skills to use. This time, my subject is none other than shy weed picker, Rhode Bennett.

I LICK THE PINK frosting from my fingers then wipe my hand with a napkin.

"Was it good?" Jorgie asks as she straightens the stack of take home menus in her new store.

I hum lightly. "*So* good. It was almost orgasmic."

She smiles brightly and moves behind the counter to straighten the rows in the display case. "I can't believe I open tomorrow. I'm so nervous," she says, leaning her hands on the glass.

"You're going to be great. I put flyers in everyone's mail boxes at work and posted all over my social media pages. I have a *really* good feeling about this."

The sound of my ringtone for my boss, Claus, permeates the air. I jump down off the counter as "Working Day and Night" by Michael Jackson plays loudly. "I have to take this."

Jorgie nods and motions in my direction as she starts to sweep the floor.

"Claus, hi! Did you get my message?"

"Yes, I did. It's a little bit of short notice to take two weeks of vacation, Joss."

"I know and I'm super sorry about that, but you see my mom is sick and I need to take care of her."

Jorgie makes a quick, disgusted snort. I narrow my eyes before turning my back to her.

"That sounds like FMLA. Maybe you should speak to Human Resources."

"No, that's not necessary. It's not a big deal. And you know what? I'd still do all my work, just from home. I'm pretty much going to be watching her sleep. I have to be there in case she needs me."

I face Jorgie again in time to see her eyes rolling at me. I give her the finger.

"But two weeks?"

"I could probably get by with one."

"Well, that sounds doable. You'll be able to finish the Frontier fact-checks and verify the info on the political piece?"

"Absolutely. It'll be no trouble at all."

"Well . . . okay then. I guess it's fine. Just make sure you have your phone on at all times in case I need you."

"Of course. Thanks, Claus."

I press end call and breathe a sigh of relief.

"You really shouldn't lie about stuff like that. Wouldn't you feel bad if Mom suddenly got sick?"

"Stop being so paranoid." I stuff my cell into my back jeans pocket. "You know I need the time off to write this article. You should see this woman. She's a nasty little thing with a horrible attitude. She's mean to everyone: her cat, me, her next door neighbor . . . I'm going to thoroughly enjoy calling her out for the fake she is. Trolls everywhere are going to fear my name and run for the hills!" I lift my hand in the air and make a fist.

Jorgie laughs.

I look around the store contently. Everything seems to be in place. "Do you need my help with anything else?"

"Did you help me with something? All I remember you doing was eating three cupcakes and watching me work."

"I meant like the moral support kind of help. I can tell you how awesome you are again if you need to hear it."

"No, I'm good." She snickers.

Pulling her in for a hug, I kiss her cheek and whisper in her ear, "You're going to be fantastic and all your dreams are going to come true."

She squeezes me tightly.

"I'll be here tomorrow right after I get done with asshole Annie. You know she lives within walking distance of here?"

"That's good. I'm sure I'm going to need that moral support by then. Mom said she's taking the day off work. She's going to be here all stinking day tomorrow. You know, in case I need her to tell me how to do it the right way."

I cringe.

"Yeah, exactly."

"I'll bring you coffee laced with booze of some kind."

"You're my angel."

I pick a piece of lint from her shirt and drop it to the ground. "I know. I'm everyone's angel." I shrug.

"Don't forget to mention how modest you are too."

I grab a cookie off the counter and sashay out the door yelling, "Love you, sissy!" into the air.

"Love you back!"

I thought of telling Jorgie about Annie's hot neighbor and all the research I did on him, but I never ever discuss men with her unless it's serious. I've only ever been serious about one guy in my life and that was in high school. I've barely said two words to Rhode Bennett, so obviously he's not worth mentioning. But damn if he isn't still on my mind for some reason.

I mentally review all I know about him as I drive back to my apartment. Rhode Bennett is the only child of Lacey and Torrance Bennett. He owns a very successful landscape company called Bennett Landscaping and he's almost thirty years old. That explains his affinity for yards. His father is a professor at a university and apparently was a Rhodes scholar, hence where Rhode got his name, I assume.

His Facebook profile was marked private, so I had to use my dummy account to friend him. I guess I could have just friended him with my real account, but I don't want to look like I'm interested in him or anything. I wish he'd accept my request. I'm dying to see more than his profile pic and cover photo. I like to know what makes people tick. You never know what info I can use to get close to him in case I need more dirt on Annie.

He's originally from Dallas and I guess his parents still live down there. I wonder if he gets lonely being up here all by himself. I was able to get his birthday and college info. He's a Sagittarius, which means he must like adventure and travel. He's also extremely compatible with me, which I find fascinating even though I have zero time for more than looking at him. Hopefully we'll get along, if I have to talk to him or anything.

I decide to play it cool next time I see him, if I see him. I mean, he has my number if he wants to talk to me, and he hasn't used it yet. Not that I've noticed. I lift my phone to make sure it's still on in case someone might be trying to reach me.

As I walk the stairs to my apartment, I start to feel bloated, probably from all the cupcakes. Even though I want to take a nap, I change my clothes and go for a run instead. I need to stay in shape in case Annie decides to chase after me on her broom when I tell the world all about her lies. Maybe it'll knock her down off her high horse a few pegs. I'll be the voice of everyone she's ever wronged. My guess is that's half this town.

After my run, I shower and put on my pajamas even though it's only seven o'clock. I grab the stack of Annie's reviews I printed from Amazon and start skimming through them.

I read the one for tissues. It got over five hundred likes. "I barely had a booger and this thing fell apart before I got it to my nose. I hate to see what would have happened if I sneezed. I probably would have blown it into party confetti complete with snot streamers. How hard is it to make a tissue? These morons probably spend all their times wiping their asses with real paper instead of the crap they make. If you like one ply, see-through, paper-thin tissues, then go ahead and buy these, or you can just burn your money. Same effect either way."

Sheesh. That was a little harsh. I wonder if she even tried them. I flip to another about a flea collar. Hmm, maybe she actually used this on her cat. Nope, she says dog. It was written last week. I'm assuming she didn't have one and get rid of it so quickly. Such a liar.

"My *dog* scratched more wearing this thing than he did before I put it on him. I actually saw bugs packing up their suitcases and telling their kids they won the lottery and were moving to a luxury resort town before they started climbing on him. All he needed was a disco ball hanging off his tail and it probably would have been a better club scene than the one at the grass where he poops. What a piece of garbage. It's made cheap and looks cheap. If you want to torture your pet and make him miserable, this is the collar for you!"

I'm not sure how many more I read before I finally doze off. In my dreams Annie is the Wicked Witch of the West from *Wizard of Oz* and is chasing me on her broom throwing products she reviewed at me from the sky. A pet rock hits me in the head and I startle awake. I guess I'm going to live and breathe this story until it's finally over. Hopefully, I make it out alive.

# CHAPTER Seven

I WONDER IF THE door is locked and whether or not I should try the handle. Will I have to listen to her berate me again if I ring the bell or knock?

I check the time on my phone. It's 9:00 a.m. on Monday morning. I did say all day, didn't I? I check my wallet to make sure I have her cash with me. I count it again. One hundred dollars a day for five days. Maybe if I wave the money in the air, she'll smell it and open the door all by herself.

I giggle to myself. As I lift my hand to the bell I stop suddenly when I hear a buzzing from the detached structure behind the house. A silver Cadillac barrels backward and comes to a screeching halt on the street.

She rolls down the window a crack and yells, "Let's go, I ain't got all day." She closes the window and faces forward.

For some reason, I feel I should run, so I do. What is it about this woman that makes me feel like she's in charge? I'm the one paying her.

I stretch out for the door handle and she drives forward a bit, causing me to reach for air. I take two steps and reach for it again. She pulls forward once more. I stop moving. "Come on!"

"You got my money with you?" she shouts through the closed window.

"Yes."

"Show me!"

I bite my lip to keep from swearing as I pull out five crisp twenty-dollar bills.

"Okay. Let's go," she says, motioning to me.

I reach for the handle one last time, promising myself I'll kick her car door if she drives forward. She doesn't. But the minute I sit down she opens her hand to me.

"My money?"

I sigh. "How about a hi, Joss? Or a can I *please* have my money?"

I stare at her for a moment and notice she's wearing a navy blue vintage feather beret hat that's tilted sideways on her head. She's dressed up today. Did someone die?

She rolls her tongue around her teeth and places her palm out directly in front of my nose. "Give me my money or get the hell out of my car."

I place the money in her hand and she spends at least five minutes checking each bill to see if it's real.

"Do you think I have a printing press in my basement or something?" I ask.

"I don't knows you. Maybe you do."

When she seems satisfied, she neatly places the bills in her wallet, making sure they're all going the same direction. She shifts the gear and her tires squeal as she presses on the gas, hard.

Reaching my hand up to the ceiling for balance, I wonder why in the hell she's driving so fast. I remember my seat belt and as I try to grab for it, she turns the corner and my face smashes against the window.

"What the fuck, Annie?" I shout.

"You should have buckled in the minute you got in the car. Only a dumbass doesn't wear a seat belt."

"I'm trying, but I can't even get to it. Are you training for the Indy 500 or are you just the worst driver in the universe?"

She slams on the brakes and I'm almost thrown into the windshield. My hands crash into the dashboard to brace for impact.

"Put on your damn belt, fool," she shouts.

I quickly buckle my seat belt and try to calm my nerves before she starts again.

"If you're gonna ride in my car you can't go making a mess." She hands me a tissue, but I'm not sure why. Am I crying on the outside? Because I know I'm screaming inside.

I take the tissue and dab my cheeks. I do feel like I'm sweating.

She rolls her eyes at me. "Get your damn hussy lipstick off my window."

Gazing at the passenger window, I can make out the outline of my face from where I hit the glass. I use the tissue to wipe away the lipstick mark and before I have a chance to face forward, the race continues.

"Where in the hell are we going?"

"The store."

"Are you late? Do they having a sale on pitchforks and you're worried you're going to miss out?"

We speed through a red light and cars all around us blow their horns.

"That was red, you know?" I yell, certain my eyes have popped out of my head.

"It just turned red. There's a five-second delay. We had plenty of time."

"Are you trying to kill me?" I hold on the door for dear life.

"Stop bitchin'! I knew you were gonna be a prissy little whiner the minute I laid eyes on you."

"Well, I knew you were going to be—" I stop myself.

"Say it. Go ahead. What's on your mind?"

She gazes over at me and stares, while she's driving. She's literally not watching the road and as she looks at me, the car veers left into oncoming traffic. Horns blare in warning.

"Annie, please! Look at the road! Oh my God!"

She faces forward and straightens out the car. "Ooh, now you're callin' on the Lord Jesus! Ain't it funny how people remember their religion in the strangest of places? You should pray more. Then you wouldn't need me to help you find God."

She doesn't even slow down when we pull into a supermarket parking lot. She finds a spot and slams on the brakes, pops it into park, and hops out of the car like nothing ever happened.

I attempt to pry my fingers from the dash, confident I've left an indentation. She's already in the store and long gone by the time I walk through the automatic door. I begin my search up and down the aisles.

I finally see her by the canned goods. She's jumping up in the air trying to reach something on the fourth shelf. I'm five-foot-six, which isn't really that tall, but she's got to be like four-foot-eight or something because she looks like a child.

I stand there watching her in amusement as she gets a running start and still can't get to whatever she's going for. I wonder how long I should let her struggle before I help her. After a few seconds I walk toward her and just as I'm about to say I'll get it, she uses the shelves like steps and catapults up two of them to reach what seems to be a can of peaches. She jumps down and lands on her feet like it's nothing. I stand there in complete disbelief. Is she part cat? She doesn't say a word. She pushes her cart and keeps walking. When I say walking, I mean what would be a sprint for a normal person. I have to hurry to reach her.

"Why are we here?"

"I need some stuff," she replies, careening her cart around various people who seem to be moving too slow for her.

"You drive a cart like you drive a car. Why are you in such a rush?"

"I got stuff to do today."

"Like what? Are you planning on reviewing something?" I can't help but feel a little excited about the idea.

"Only if something pisses me off. Speaking of that, what kind of lipstick are you wearing?"

"Umm, I don't know. Why? Do you want some?"

"Ha. No. I don't wear Scarlet Slut. But if I keep having to look at it on your narrow little mouth all day, I might be so inclined to tell someone what I think of it."

I stop in my tracks. Is that how it works? She writes reviews for things she doesn't like? I jog to catch up to her by the cold cuts. "Do you only write reviews for things you hate?"

"I never said that."

"So sometimes you say positive things?"

"Didn't say that either."

She rounds a corner and walks into the liquor department. I think it's a mistake until she places a bottle of scotch in her cart.

"Having a party?"

"There you go again making assumptions. It's none of your business."

We get up to the register to check out. Two cans of peaches, a pound of turkey, and a bottle of booze. What an odd combination. She uses one crisp twenty to pay for it. I'm worried I'm never going to get anything out of her at this rate.

As we head toward the car, I ponder how far it would be if I walked. "Would you like me to drive?" I ask, almost begging her with my eyes.

"Do you have a car here?"

"At the grocery store? Well, no."

"Then how are you going to drive?"

"I meant drive your car."

"Child, you have a screw loose if you think I'd let you behind the wheel of my caddy."

Knowing I don't have a choice, I quickly buckle myself in the seat, close my eyes, and hold on for dear life. After a few seconds I hear a tap on the window.

"If you're going to sit in there all day, maybe I

should crack a window for you."

Opening one eye, I notice Annie staring at me. I open the door. "Aren't we leaving?"

She shakes her head, places the bottle and cans in the car, and starts walking down the street with the turkey. I'm insanely curious now. Everything she does is so unpredictable.

We walk a block and she stops in front of a gray, broken-down house.

"Now you listen to me. I expect you to be a fly on the wall. You wanted to see what I do and all you're gonna do is watch. Understand? As far as she's concerned you're deaf and mute."

"She?"

"If you can't be quiet then you can go back to the car. Or better yet, you can go home."

I zip my lips.

She climbs the stairs and walks into the house without knocking. She must have a thing against it.

"I'm here," she shouts, kicking off her shoes and motioning for me to do the same. "Don't pay attention to the cornflake following me around. She wants to watch me."

Why must she insult me every second? I can hear a television playing in the back room, but no one responds. Annie walks into the kitchen, opens a cabinet, pulls out some bread, and begins unwrapping the turkey from the store. I wonder if anyone lives here. At this point I wouldn't be surprised if Annie is legit insane.

She makes a sandwich and pours a cup of milk, then wanders to the back of the house. There's a woman sitting in a chair dozing. I think. She could be dead.

Annie puts the plate and cup on the end table and shouts, "Thea!" clapping her hands.

The woman startles awake. "Whatchoo yelling 'bout?"

"I had to yell. You didn't hear me come in?"

"What?"

Annie searches left and right around the chair, bends down, and places something in Thea's ear. "Now can you hear me?"

The woman lifts a finger to her ear and twists it. She nods as Annie pulls a tray table over to her and places the sandwich in front of her.

"Did you eat breakfast?" she asks.

"Yeah, I had an egg."

"What kinda egg?"

"Poached."

"You a liar! You ain't ever poached an egg in your life!"

Annie picks up a sweater off the floor and starts folding it. I stand by the entrance trying to figure out why we're here. I wonder if they're sisters.

"I was watching that Masterchef Junior show and those little 'ems were doing it. If they can so can I." She starts swirling her hand in a circle. "You get the water going real fast like a tornado and you drop it and it swirls and shit."

"You ain't gonna poach nothin'."

"I'm tellin' you. When you come back I'm gonna make you an egg." She turns her head slightly and does a double take at me. She holds her hand up next to her mouth. "Annie, don't look now, but there's a blonde bimbo in my family room."

Annie waves. "She ain't nothin'."

"You don't see her? Shit. I'm hallucinatin', Annie. Call the doctor. I think I'm dyin'!"

"You aren't dying, Thea. Shut your face. I see her. I meant just ignore her. She's following me around 'cause she thinks I'm important."

"She mute?"

"I wish she were. I told her to keep her mouth shut."

Thea stares at me with big eyes and takes a bite of her sandwich. It's like she's waiting for me to move. I know people probably talk about me behind my back, but in front of my face is strange to say the least. I open my mouth to speak and Annie snaps her fingers at me.

I wrinkle my nose.

"Ooh, you told her. You gots her trained." Thea starts to laugh.

"What do you need?" Annie asks.

"Nothin'."

"You got some laundry for me?"

"Uh-huh. By the door."

"All right. I'm going. I'll see you soon. Lock that door when I leave."

Annie kisses her on the top of the head and Thea takes a sip of milk before changing the TV channel.

Annie picks up a bag and marches out the door. I follow as usual. When I catch up to her she's already at the car and is placing the bag in the trunk.

I watch her and wonder if she's going to volunteer the information or if I'm going to have to ask.

She opens the car door and starts the ignition. I bolt into the car and put on my belt. I guess we're leaving now.

"She a friend. That's all I'm gonna say. Understand?"

I nod and prepare for the race home. They kind of looked alike. I wonder if they really are sisters and she doesn't want to tell me. I think of Jorgie and my promise to bring her liquor tonight. I glance over my shoulder at the bottle of scotch rolling around on the floor. I almost wish that bottle were mine. It might help get through this day.

# CHAPTER Eight

I THOUGHT I'D STAY with Annie until at least five, but at four I decide I've had enough. I spent the day watching her do laundry, a crossword puzzle, and doze off to *Jeopardy.* She barely spoke to me after we left Thea and she ignored my requests to discuss her reviews. She was downright rude. I should have left when she made herself a sandwich and didn't offer me anything. I didn't even get a glass of water. I'm defeated and hungry. What a waste of a day. I'm trudging to my car as Rhode pulls into his driveway.

I might be happy to see him if I wasn't in the worst mood ever.

He waves to me happily and I offer a nod. How does he live by her and stay positive? I spent a few hours with her and I feel like it was a few months. I sit in my car and rest my head on my steering wheel. I feel like someone drained all the life out of my body.

A tap on my window causes me to jump. I panic thinking Annie has returned for round two. But it's not Annie, it's Rhode, and he's a sight for sore eyes. I turn the key in the ignition and open the window.

"You okay?" he asks with a smile.

"How do you do it? Is there a magic potion you could share?"

"You spent the day with Annie, huh?" he questions, crouching down next to my window.

I nod. Tears threaten my eyes.

His face is etched with concern. He opens his mouth to say something and seems to stop himself. He glances up at her house, then down the street. "Would you like to go for a walk with me?"

I gaze backwards in the direction he's pointing and decide he could be just what I need right now. He's a perfect distraction. I nod again and open my door. He holds out his hand to help me out of the car. I like the way my hand feels inside his. He's tough and tender at the same time. He's dressed in khakis and a button-down dress shirt today. He's hot cleaned up, but I think he's even hotter dirty. How is that possible?

"You might want to take your key," he says when I all but abandon everything.

"Ugh, thanks. I'm not myself today."

"Rough day?"

"If being called a slut, a hussy, a twig, a cornflake, a whiner, and annoying isn't rough enough, how about sticking your head under the sink just for a drink of water? At least she puts a bowl out for the cat."

He cringes. "She doesn't mean to be that way."

"Oh yes, she does! She means every word of it. She even snapped her fingers at me to get me to be quiet."

"Did it work?"

I lean on my car. "Yes! I'm scared of her."

He laughs and it warms me from my toes upward.

"I'm not keeping you from anything, am I? I feel bad that you have to console me."

"Not at all. I was actually going to walk into town and grab dinner. I've been sitting behind a desk all day and I'm stir-crazy. Is it safe to assume that if you didn't get water, you also didn't have food?"

"It's safe. I haven't eaten all day."

"Would you want to join me?" He rubs the back of his neck nervously.

I don't get the shyness. He's beautiful. Surely women must throw themselves at him constantly.

"I'd love to. Do you mind if we make a couple of stops along the way?"

"Not at all. I have time."

We start walking and I'm already feeling better.

"What do you do?" I ask, even though I already know.

"I work at a landscape company."

He works at one? Why wouldn't he admit he owns it? "Oh, does Annie pay you to cut her grass?"

"Nah. I enjoy it, so I do it even though she tells me not to. As you saw yesterday."

"And you bring her dinner?"

"Every night."

I stop walking and stare at him.

He takes a few more steps and turns to face me. "You think I'm crazy, don't you?"

"Every night? Why can't you be my neighbor?"

He smiles, shrugs, and walks backward for a bit until I'm next to him again. "I feel bad for her. She's all alone. I don't think she has a lot of money."

"Yeah, I got that feeling too. Especially when her

hand was in my face and she said, 'Where's my money?'"

He shakes his head. "She's not making a very good impression on you, is she? I hope you'll get to know her before you start the article. Just know she means the opposite of what she says."

"Oh, so when she called me a hussy she really meant I was a sweet, good girl?"

"Exactly," he says, motioning with his hand.

"So I guess when she called me skinny, she really meant I was fat then too?"

"No. Not that. You're perfect."

I can't help the smile that spreads across my face like a Cheshire cat.

"Ahh." He shakes his head at himself and stuffs his hands into his pockets.

"You think I'm perfect?" I'm not letting this chance go. "Why, Rhode, are you flirting with me?"

His phone rings. "Excuse me, please. I need to get this. Hello? Yes, hi, how are you? Okay. Yes. Really? I'd rather not. Okay. Yes. No problem. Tacos? About an hour? Absolutely. All right, see you soon."

He ends the call and stuffs his cell into his pocket.

"I guess I'll take a rain check on that dinner," I say, noting someone obviously wants to meet with him.

"Why?"

I point to his pocket. "The call. I assume you have plans?"

"Oh no. That was Annie." He pauses and rubs his hand over the back of his neck. "She, uh, wanted to let me know she saw me walk off with you and that if you didn't move your car in the next hour, she's going to have it towed."

I roll my eyes and cross my arms. "And yet you feed her?"

He shrugs. "I'd be happy to feed you as well. It's the least I can do to make up for how mean she was to you today."

"I'll make you a deal. You buy me dinner and I'll get dessert."

"Done!"

I glance to the left and the right. "Do you mind if I make a quick stop here?" I ask, pointing to a liquor store.

His brows furrow. I can tell he's curious. "That bad, huh?"

"You don't even know."

He follows me as I run to the counter and grab a mini bottle of Kahlua. When we leave the store I point to a coffee shop and he follows me again. When I pour the bottle inside the coffee, he smiles. I close the lid and I think he expects me to take a sip. I feel I should explain.

I point down the street to my sister's bakery. There are cars lined up in front of it and I can't hide my excitement. "Do you see that bakery down there?"

"Oh yeah. It opened today, didn't it? What a great addition to the neighborhood."

I swear I like him more and more every second. "It's my little sister's. My mom has been there all day. She texted me six times asking me to save her. As bad as Annie is, my mother is a force of her own right. Jorgie probably needs this more than I do. Are you okay if we stop by there before dinner?"

"Sure. I'm guessing she prefers her coffee on the warm side. It's nice that you have family close by and a sibling. I'm an only child and my family is out of state. I guess you could say Annie is the only family I have."

I hold out the cup of coffee. "Here. You win. I think you beat us all."

He laughs. "I don't drink coffee."

I do a double take at him. "Is there something wrong with you?"

"Probably," he says with a smile.

I face him for a moment and the way he's looking at me makes me tingly all over. What is it about this guy? As we continue to walk, my mind is flooded with questions. The reporter in me takes over. I have to know things.

"Do you think your girlfriend will mind you buying me dinner?"

He licks his lips and smiles. He knows I'm fishing, but I don't care.

"Are you asking if I have a girlfriend?"

"Yes. Do you?"

"Not yet, but I'm working on it. You know someone?"

"That depends. Are you the hearts and flowers type of guy? The 'where are you and why haven't you texted me back' guy? Or the guy who just likes an occasional bang?"

His head jerks back and his lips part. "Wow. Are you always so direct?"

"Yes. So?"

"I'd say on a given day I could be any one of them."

I smirk. He's confident right now and I'm loving

his playfulness. We stop right outside my sister's bakery. "So, what I hear you saying is you suffer from multiple personality disorder?"

He leans in a bit and whispers, "Would you like to find out?"

Holy fucksticks! Who is this man and what happened to shy lawnmower boy? I open my mouth to speak and the chimes ring as Jorgie's bakery door opens suddenly. A hand grabs my arm.

"You'd better have liquor."

I turn and hug a smiling, slightly frazzled Jorgie. I hand her the coffee. "Kahlua seemed like a good choice."

She takes a sip and moans lightly in pleasure. I glance over at Rhode and his lip curls into a crooked smile.

"Jorgie, this is Rhode, Annie's neighbor. Rhode, this is my sister, Jorgie."

Jorgie holds out her hand. "Hi. Oh, I love your name. I bet you get jokes about being named after a street, don't you?"

He shakes her hand. "You could say it wasn't an easy name to grow up with."

"How's it spelled?" she asks.

"R-h-o-d-e."

"Like a scholar?"

He smiles brightly and their eyes lock. "My father was one. That's very astute of you. Most people don't get the connection from the spelling."

"Don't let the flour in my hair fool you. I know things."

I glance back and forth between them, feeling I

need to regain control. "Where's Mom?"

"Can you please make her leave? Take her with you?"

I hold up my hands. "I said I'd bring you a drink. What you're asking for would have to be three years' worth of birthday and Christmas presents combined."

"Joslyn! It's nice of you to finally grace us with your presence. You knew this was a big day for your sister." She regards the cup in Jorgie's hand as she marches out the bakery door. "Why in God's name would you bring her coffee? You know she sells her own coffee here. That's bad for business."

My mother's voice makes my ears hurt. I open my mouth to speak and she continues.

"It's almost five o'clock. It's just like you to avoid having to help out. Where have you been?"

"Hi, Mom. Good to see you too. And so you know, I was working."

"In jeans? Is casual Monday a thing now?"

Jorgie scoots around her slyly, trying to avoid being drawn into the conversation. She slips back into the store, sipping her drink the whole way.

"I'm on an assignment."

She rolls her eyes and offers a fake smile. "I didn't know fact-checkers got to leave the office."

I loathe her for trying to make me look bad. Even though I rarely care what people think, she could ruin my cover if I don't respond. "My editor thinks I have potential. I got the okay for an article submission, not that I need to explain myself to you."

Rhode holds out his hand and my mother takes it, not letting go while he speaks. "Mrs. Walters, it's so nice to meet you. I'm a friend of your daughter. I've heard a lot about you."

"Oh, I bet you have. Are you her assignment?" She's still holding his hand when her head turns to me. "Are you doing an article on sex objects?"

I can't even pretend to be surprised by her question. Rhode's cheeks might be a slight shade of pink. He's probably in shock. I guess now he knows why I say whatever I feel. I learned it from my mother. Nothing she says takes me off guard anymore. "Yes, Mother. I took a side job at *Playgirl* and Rhode is Mr. September."

Rhode takes his hand back from Jane Walters' vice grip and runs his fingers awkwardly through his hair.

"I would have said June myself. You'd do well to snag yourself a man like him."

I sigh. "Oh, don't worry, Mother. I'm going to take him in Jorgie's back room and shag him on the frosting table."

Rhode's eyes bulge and his mouth falls open.

"Honestly, be a lady," she says while shaking her head.

She's such a hypocrite.

"Well, it's nice to meet you. I'm sorry my daughter is so crude and rude. Joslyn, why are you making this poor man stand out in the heat when your sister has air conditioning? Rhode, is it?"

Rhode nods. I'm guessing he's afraid to speak.

"Let's get you something cool to drink. Jorgie has smoothies. Do you like smoothies?" She wraps her arm in his and leads him into the store. He gazes over his shoulder at me and I mouth "I'm sorry," to him.

His returning smile makes my vajayjay squirm. I actually *would* bang him on the frosting table. I'm pretty sure I'd bang him anywhere, come to think of it.

# CHAPTER Nine

I YAWN AS I hop up the stairs to Annie's house. I was up extra early this morning, forging a plan on how to crack her. Even though my hands are full, I manage to turn Annie's door handle. It's not locked, so I walk in, taking one last glance at Rhode's house as I enter.

I never did get to have dinner with him last night. My mother demanded I take her home and Rhode said he understood. I think I saw him run away from the bakery. I'm sure all things Walters scare him now.

"So now you just walk in? You think you live here or something?" Annie shouts from the kitchen. "You're lucky I don't have a gun or I might shoot you for trespassing."

"Good morning, Annie," I say in my most chipper voice, determined to not get frustrated today. I place my duffle bag on the floor and walk to the back of the house.

She's sitting at the kitchen table reading her newspaper when I place two cups of coffee and a bag of my sister's freshly baked muffins on her table.

"What's this?"

"I thought maybe I'd bring breakfast."

"If you think for one second this food means you don't have to pay me, you best be hightailing your flaky butt outta here."

I pull Annie's money from my back pocket and place it on the table.

"Eww. You had it stuffed in your pocket? Now it probably smells like ass."

I shrug. "Money is money, right? Plus, I made them fresh in my basement this morning."

"Along with these disgusting muffins, I assume?" She sniffs the bag and waves her hand in front of her face like they're rotten.

I close my eyes briefly and count to ten. I can do this today. "They're from that new bakery that opened in town. They're actually quite delish. Have you heard of the place?" I ask, wondering if she'll admit to her nasty review.

She lifts her head to read the name on the bag. "Nope. Never heard of them."

She holds each twenty up to the light as usual and takes her sweet time making sure they're all real.

"I got your coffee black," I tell her.

"Oh, you think 'cause I'm old I like everything boring?"

I dump out the sugar, fake sugar, creamer, half and half, and flavored creamers on the table. "I didn't know *how* you took it, so I got a little of everything."

"You clean out the place? Whatchoo gonna do with all this? Open a condiment store?"

I shrug as I open my coffee lid and proceed to dump three vanilla flavored cream cups inside along with two packets of sugar. As I'm stirring it, I notice Annie staring at me.

"You like coffee with your crap? Why you bother to get coffee at all if you're gonna ruin it with all that junk?"

She takes a sip of hers. Black. I want to make a comment, but I choose to keep my mouth shut.

"Do you want blueberry or chocolate chip?" I ask as I remove two muffins from the bag.

"Did you poison them?"

"No. I'm saving the poison for the last day, after I write my article."

I almost think I see a twinkle in her eye.

I gaze out her back window. "Did Rhode bring you tacos last night?"

"Yeah, they were cold, thanks to you. Why?"

"I just wondered. How did he seem?"

Her eyes narrow and she takes a bite of the blueberry muffin. "He seemed irritating as usual." She places the muffin on the table and stares at me for a second. "You into him?"

"Me? No! Not at all."

"Uh-huh. I saw you two walking last night. You were making googly eyes at him."

"I was not. I don't even know what googly eyes are."

"Oh yeah, you do. You made 'em." Her voice rises an octave as she speaks in what I assume is supposed to be an imitation of me. "Oh, Rhode, you is such a manly man. My kitty has been ignored for so long. Would you like to pet it and hear it meow?"

I almost spit my coffee. I think she thinks I'll be

angry, but I laugh instead. "Would it be so bad if I liked him?"

"I expect it. Annoying attracts annoying. Maybe you can get him to leave me alone and he can get you to go away."

"I don't think he'll go anywhere. He really likes you. You must be nicer to him than you are to me." I chuckle lightly.

She makes a face as she takes another bite of her muffin. "These are lousy and the coffee is mediocre." She spits her food into a napkin and gets up to throw it in the trash.

I shake my head. They're fantastic. She ate over half of it before she said she didn't like it. It makes me think she complains just to complain.

"Stupid, come eat your breakfast."

She opens a can and places a bowl on the table. "Want me to get some for you too?" she says with a small laugh.

"Ha-ha."

My chair shakes and I hear a thump as Stupid runs into it. "Aww. You okay?"

"You ain't supposed to be here. He's confused."

I pick him up and place him on the table to eat his food.

"Get your stuff, we gotta go," Annie announces.

"Where are we going now?" I ask, slightly afraid to get in a car with Annie again.

"Work. You gonna make me late."

"Work? You have a job?"

"Why you so shocked? Yeah, I got a job."

I'm secretly surprised anyone would hire her. "Can

I drive?"

"You gonna expect me to pay for your gas?"

"No."

"Okay then, let's go." She motions to the door. I grab my bag and my coffee and hustle over to my car to make sure my passenger seat is still clean. I heard enough from my mother about my messy car yesterday to last me a lifetime. I don't need to hear anything from Annie.

I open the door and she gazes into the back seat at the wrappers, clothes, shoes, and take-out bags. She slides into the seat and clutches her purse tightly to her chest. She buckles her seat belt and slowly glances behind her one more time before staring at me in awe. She starts making that noise with her teeth.

"I know. It's a mess. I don't need to hear it."

"Child, you homeless? You livin' in your car?"

"No! I'm not homeless. I'm just not very organized."

"Organized ain't the word I'd use. You probably got bugs livin' in here."

"No. I don't. I cleaned it a couple of days ago. Now where are we going?"

She motions straight and gazes over the seat one more time. "I don't like this."

"What? Are you afraid my driving will be too slow for you?" I laugh.

"There could be a dead body back there."

Rolling my eyes, I drink what's left of my coffee and toss the empty cup over my shoulder.

"You did not!"

"What?"

"Throw your cup in your back seat. That's a disgrace. You need to take care of your things. Turn here."

I drive as instructed. "I do."

"No, you don't. You gotta have respect for your things. Just like people. It goes a long way."

I gaze over at her and ponder her choice of words. They're almost exactly mine. Could she and I have something in common? She seems really nervous. Have I found her weakness? Is it possible Annie hates chaos?

She motions for me to turn into the parking lot of a dollar store.

"You work here?"

"Yeah. You got a problem with that?"

"No. I just didn't expect you to work with . . . well . . . you know, people. Since you hate them so much."

"I don't hate people. I hate annoying little twerps that don't listen. Now, you can't stay. Harold isn't going to want you bothering me. Come back and get me at two."

"Two?" I question. "No way. Our deal was all day."

"You ain't gonna get me fired. Now skedaddle."

I watch her walk into the store in complete disbelief. She let me drive her here and then expects me to come back in four hours to get her? I was trying so hard to keep my cool, but I'm starting to get angry. I place the gear in reverse and change my mind. She can't tell me what to do. It's a public place. I'll just go in there and look around.

As soon as I walk through the door I notice another older woman working at the register. She smiles. Clearly Annie doesn't work the register. I hope. How could anyone be dumb enough to place Annie in a job dealing with the public? Better yet, who in their right mind would hire her?

I sashay up and down the aisles looking for Annie. I start to wonder if she ran out a back door to escape me. This is a big store. It's clean and organized. I can see why she likes it. Pretty colors and items I didn't know I needed distract me. One dollar for lotion? Why do I not shop here?

Before I know it, I can no longer hold all my purchases. I drop a can of Pringles and a nice man bends to get it for me.

"Would you like a cart?" he asks.

"You have carts?" It's as if the heavens opened.

He smiles brightly. "Give me a second."

I'm so excited I almost forget why I'm in the store in the first place. That is, until I see his name badge—Harold.

"Here you go, sweetheart."

"You're Harold. Annie's boss?"

"Oh boy." His eyes roll. "What did she do?"

I like him even more. "Nothing. Well, not yet." I drop all my items into the cart and hold out my hand to him. "I'm Joss. I'm writing an article on her for *The Gaggle*."

"The magazine?"

"The one and only. I'm supposed to be following her around all day to write a story. She told me I couldn't come in, but I didn't listen." I wink at him.

"Of course you can come in." He glances down at the items in my cart.

"Is it okay if I hang out here and watch her? I promise to stay out of the way. I'll just be shopping."

He gently touches my arm. "Any friend of Annie's is a friend of mine. You are more than welcome to stay. Let me know if you need anything."

"She isn't my friend."

I hear her voice before I see her.

"Annie, did you really tell this nice girl she couldn't shop here?" Harold asks.

I smirk and cross my arms.

"No. She didn't say anything about spending money. I told her she couldn't loiter and follow me around. I said I had work to do."

"She's writing an article for *The Gaggle* on you? What did you do?"

"Some people like me."

He turns to me. "If you find something nice to say about Annie, any chance you could mention the store?" Harold asks, wringing his hands.

"I don't see why not."

Annie places her hands on her hips. "Whatchoo mean *if* she finds something nice to say about me?"

Harold ignores her, waving his hand in the air. "Then you are more than welcome here, Joss. As a matter of fact, Annie, you should show her around."

"My cart—"

"Oh, I'll hold it for you. Go ahead and grab anything else you'd like. Annie, do whatever she wants."

Annie frowns and I grin until my entire face is a smile. This day keeps getting better.

As soon as Harold walks away Annie crosses her arms. "You is trouble."

"No, I'm not. I'm sweet and fun. You just haven't

bothered to get to know me."

"You're a pain in the ass. That's what you are."

Annie stomps away mumbling something under her breath. Harold took my cart and Annie left me. I'm not sure whether or not I'm supposed to follow her, but seeing as she never tells me, I decide I'd better.

She wanders through an employees only entrance, but I go after her, certain my new buddy Harold wouldn't mind.

She's still talking to herself when she bends down and picks up a box twice her size and tosses it like it's made of air.

"Hey. Where's my tour?" I ask. I know I'm pushing it, but I don't care. It's fun.

"You want a tour? Come here."

I follow her down a hall to a door. "Inside here is where magic happens. Go see for yourself."

I push the door and a light flickers above a dirty toilet. "Seriously?"

"Go see what's written on the sign on the back of the door."

I step inside and she pulls the door closed so I can see it. There's nothing on the door. Then I hear a click.

"Annie? There's no sign in here." I pull on the handle and it's locked. "Annie?"

"Oooh, no sign? Hmm. Someone must have stolen it. I wonder who. Enjoy your visit." She laughs.

"What? Oh come on! We were just playing." The lights go out in the bathroom and I freak out. "Annie, it's dark!"

"It's motion activated, you big dodo bird. Wave your hands around. Get comfortable. I'll be back in a few hours. Nobody tells me what to do. Tour my ass."

"You can't be serious. Annie? Annie?"

After a few minutes of silence I realize she's not coming back. "What the actual fuck?" I yell for help and there's no response. I realize I'm in the back of the store room and no one can hear me. Unless some-one has to poop in the near future I'm stuck back here. What if there were a fire? What kind of bathroom door locks from the outside?

Annie isn't only angry. She's also devious. I'm guessing she doesn't like being told what to do and she certainly doesn't like being teased. The lights go out again and I wave my arms around like a bird flapping its wings. I remove my purse from around my neck and place it on the sink. My purse!

I take out my cell and begin searching for the phone number for the store. If I tell Harold what Annie did, would he fire her? As much as I like the idea of getting her in trouble, I'm certain that if I tattle, she'll be done with me. I still need those reviews.

I place my phone in my back pocket and gaze up at fluorescent lights. That's when I see a vent above the toilet. A light bulb flicks on in my head. I think back to all the movies I've seen where people escape through vents. It can't be that hard, right? It seems wide enough. I imagine myself climbing through the vents and scaring Annie on the other side. The idea of freaking her out gives me sick pleasure.

I wonder if I step on the toilet if I can reach it. The toilet is nasty, so I layer toilet paper on the bowl so I don't get the bottom of my Chucks dirty. I carefully step up and lift my arms above my head. I'm still too far away.

Think, Joss, think. As I'm staring around the room, the lights go out again. I need to keep moving. Hopping off the toilet, I pace for a bit before staring at my reflection in the mirror. I turn around and lean on the sink. What can I use to give me more height? There isn't much in the room other than the waste paper basket. That's it! I'll stand on the basket on the toilet. Sounds like a good plan to me.

I dump the trash on the floor and turn the basket upside down on the paper lined toilet. I slowly step from the bowl to the basket and can finally reach the vent. With one hand on the wall and the other on the vent, I dig my nails under the edge and start to pull. The lights go out again. Afraid to lose what little progress I've made, I release my hand from the wall and wave.

I hear a cracking noise and I pray my gut is wrong. "No, please!"

The waste basket cracks under my full body weight and my foot slips right through it and directly into the water with a giant splash.

"Fucking fuck!"No!"

I want to cry. It hurts, but more than that I'm mortified. I try to lift my foot out of the toilet and it's stuck. It's lodged in the bowl. Is this how it ends? I can see the bi-line, "Aspiring journalist dies of starvation in dollar store bathroom. Found with one foot inside a dirty toilet bowl with a garbage can around her leg."

Just as I'm about to scream bloody murder, my phone vibrates in my back pocket. It's an unknown number. Oh God. What if it's Claus calling from home?

I almost reject the call, but at this point, I feel as if

someone should hear me take my last breath.

"Hello?" I try not to seem panicked.

"Joss? Hey, it's Rhode. Is this a bad time?"

"Oh, Rhode!" My voice is almost a whimper. "Thank God you called! I've never been so glad to hear your voice."

"Well, damn. I was kind of hoping you'd be happy to hear from me, but this exceeded my expectations."

"I need help!"

"What's going on? Are you okay?"

"No. No, I'm not. Annie locked me in a bathroom at her workplace and I've had a little accident."

"Wait, what? What kind of accident? Are you hurt?"

"Umm, I'm kinda okay and kinda not."

"Stay there. I'm on my way."

"I couldn't go anywhere if I tried."

"Umm, where am I going? I didn't know Annie had a job."

"Yeah, she works at the dollar store over on Fifth."

"Okay, I'll leave now. I'll be there in twenty minutes, give or take traffic. Unless, you want me to call someone else. Like the police or fire department first?"

"No. Please don't tell anyone."

"Okay, I'll be right there. Do you want to stay on the phone?"

An image of Rhode walking into the bathroom and seeing me with my foot stuck in the toilet bowl plays like a movie in my head. Is this how I want him to think of me from here on out? I bet I smell like literal shit. "Wait!" I shout. "Don't come. Do me a favor and call Annie. Tell her to let me out. Please?"

"Are you sure?"

"Yes. If she doesn't come, then I'll call you back."

"All right, I'll call her now. And, Joss? I'm going to talk to her about this."

"Thanks. Just call her, okay?"

I stand there for what seems like forever. The lights go out again and I no longer have the energy to wave my hands. I position myself as comfortably as possible while toilet water creeps up my jeans. I wonder how many people have crapped in this toilet and how many anti-disease shots I'm going to have to get if I ever get out. I think of all the possibilities to keep my mind occupied. There's tetanus, hepatitis, rabies . . .

Just as I'm about to call Rhode back, the bathroom door flies open. Annie takes one look at me as the lights flicker to life and covers her mouth with her hand. A snicker turns into a full-blown howl.

"You know what?" I scream. "I could have called the police on you, or called Harold for that matter, but I didn't. Because I'm a good person."

"You tryin' to convince me or yourself?" She walks toward me and looks in the bowl. "Child, what did you do? I told you to wait. Did you try to flush yourself down the toilet?"

"No, I tried to climb up the garbage can to reach the vent so I could climb out. It cracked and I fell in and now my foot is stuck."

"Some might say you're in a real shitty situation."

"So help me God, Annie!"

"I don't know 'bout you, but I'm pooped." She slaps her hand on her leg as she continues to laugh.

"It isn't funny! I'm really stuck. Stop laughing at

me. I'm tired of all of this."

"You tired of taking everybody's crap?" She roars at that one.

My bottom lip quivers. I'm going to die here with the worst joke teller in history.

"Ooh, now don't cry. No sense losing any more water." She leans over me and seems to assess the situation. "Well, just pull your foot out of the toilet."

My head leans to the side in disbelief. "Don't you think I would have done that if I could?"

"How in the world?" she asks as she lifts the garbage can up my leg. "It looks like your shoe is stuck. Maybe if you slide your foot out of your shoe you'll be okay."

"I can't slide it out. My shoes are tied tight."

"Then untie them."

"I can't reach." I show her how I can barely bend because of the trash can. "You need to do it."

"Nu-uh. I ain't sticking my hands in that bowl. I'm pretty sure Harold shit out a month's worth of pork chops in there this morning."

I put my hands over my eyes. "You're not helping me."

"I didn't force you to go swimming."

"Annie. Please!"

She stares at me for a moment and starts making that clicking sound in her mouth again. "Hold on. I gots an idea."

I sigh and watch her leave. So help me, she'd better come back. A minute later, she returns with salad tongs. She starts unwrapping them from the plastic.

"Are you serious? You're going to use dollar store

salad tongs to get me out of the toilet? What's wrong with you?"

"Shut your face. You want my help or not?"

I nod.

"Hold your designer basket legging up."

I lift the basket and she plunges the tongs into the water and starts working them around my shoe.

"Do you have any idea how much I paid for these shoes? I'm never going to be able to wear them again, you know?"

"Hush your mouth. Your breath stinks and I can't focus on your shoe with your skunk breath in my face."

I wrinkle my nose and breathe into my hand to try to smell my breath. It seems fine to me.

She leans on me for leverage. "Try to pull on three. One, two, three!"

Nothing happens. She repositions herself and places one foot on the toilet for support. "Now listen here, when I say three, we both gonna twist and pull."

The bathroom door opens and the woman from the front register walks in. Annie and I both turn and stare at her. Her mouth drops open.

"Don't you know how to knock? Can't you see we busy?"

She pivots on her heel.

"Okay, on three," Annie says.

I can't help but laugh at how ridiculous we must have looked and how quickly she walked away. Does Annie do this thing a lot?

"Oh, now you wanna laugh? I'm not supposed to laugh, but now you gonna start?"

"Just say three, Annie."

"One, two, three!"

We both almost fall to floor as my foot pops out of the toilet. My shoe is still lodged inside.

Annie stares at the tongs in her hand. "Imagine what they could do to a salad."

My leg is soaked and my sock is dirty. I want to hurl. I remove the basket from my leg and grab the tongs from Annie's hand to remove my sock. It only takes me a moment to free my shoe, but I know I never want to see them again.

"Now what am I supposed to do?"

"Stop your whining. I'll be right back."

I hobble over to the sink and immediately remove my jeans. I begin the process of washing my leg with the hand soap. I wonder if these jeans are even salvageable.

Annie returns with flip-flops and a pair of scissors. "I got you pink 'cause you like girly shit."

She picks up my jeans.

"Wait! What are you doing?" I shout.

"You wanna walk through the store in your skivvies?"

"My what?"

"Your . . ." Her head turns to the side to study my thong. Can I be any more uncomfortable?

"If you want to walk out of here in your dental floss, then that's up to you, but I got work to do. Am I cutting or not?"

My chest feels heavy as I wave at her. "Cutting."

She starts to work on the material. "These are some of the worst scissors I've ever seen in my life. I bet they couldn't cut a piece of paper if they tried."

I turn my head away. I can't watch her destroy my favorite jeans. I sniff and rub my nose.

"Oh, now stop making such a fuss. You know what I always say, if life hands you lemons—"

"Let me guess. You make lemonade."

She stops cutting and eyeballs me. "Didn't your momma ever teach you it's rude to interrupt? Have some manners. Now I got to start all over." She shakes her head. Can she be any worse?

"If life gives you lemons, you cut 'em in half and squeeze 'em in people's eyes so they can't see you coming."

I snort. "What's that supposed to mean?"

"Oh, child. Don't you know nothin'? Life is hard. Bad things happen. Now you can take the bad and live with it, or you can use the bad as a way to build again. Show that bad it doesn't own you. You come back strong. You find a way to make life work."

She hands me my jeans. "Now, put on some stinkin' clothes. You're making me feel like I got something in my teeth and need to floss." Annie turns her back to me and I try not to smile.

I pull on my new jean shorts. They're actually kind of cute in a homemade sort of way. They show off my thigh muscles. I slide on my pink flip-flops and toss my shoes in the broken waste paper basket.

Annie turns around and holds out her hand. "Salad tongs, flip-flops, and scissors. That's three dollars and change. Pay up."

I'm fairly certain I've been handed an entire bag of lemons in the form of Annie McClintonuck. I guess I need to figure out how to squeeze them in her eyes. I refuse to admit to myself that even with all her flaws, she's smart and funny. I might like her a little bit. No, it can't be. I won't let her grow on me. I won't.

# Chapter Ten

ANNIE POUNDS ON MY window and I'm startled awake. I unlock the door and move my dollar purchases to the back seat. She wipes off the seat and hesitantly climbs inside. After I left the bathroom, I finished my shopping and paid for all my things, including the salad tongs I threw in the garbage as I left.

I ate a can of chips and a bag of gummy worms before I dozed off in my car. Looks like Annie is ready to go home. Stretching my arms in front of me, I yawn and put the car in drive.

Annie glances at my back seat mess and shakes her head. "You know it wouldn't take long to clean it."

"I know."

"Why do you throw all your crap back there? Don't you have garbage cans where you live?"

"It's really bothering you, isn't it?"

"Yes."

"Good."

"That's how you gonna play, huh? All right, then. I guess I won't share my review idea then." She crosses her arms and leans back into the seat.

My head jerks to look at her. "You have a review for me?"

"I might have had one if your car were clean."

"I'm paying you one hundred dollars a day for information on your review process and now you're telling me in addition to that money, I also have to clean my car?"

"All I'm saying is that maybe I'd think more clearly if I didn't worry you murdered someone and hid the body under that trash."

Pulling the car in front of her home, I turn off the ignition and glance behind me at my back seat. "If I clean my car, I get a review?"

She shrugs before strolling toward her house.

I open my car door and shout, "I'm going to need a garbage bag!"

Her front door opens and she throws out a box of trash bags before she closes the door.

I spend the next hour cleaning my entire car. I find three bottles of nail polish I forgot I had, two pairs of boots, a sweater, a half-eaten turkey sandwich that grew mold, two cell phone chargers I thought I'd lost, and the notebook I used last year to write down all the rejected ideas I presented to Darla. I fill up two big bags and toss them in Annie's bin before wandering back into her house, exhausted but proud.

"Okay, it's done. Want to see?"

Annie's eyes are closed and she's slumped in her chair in front of the TV. I stand there for a few minutes, watching her cautiously. Is she breathing? Her chest isn't moving, so I place a finger under her nose. When

I feel hot air, I'm reminded she's full of it.

Slightly relieved my article subject hasn't gone to hell, I plop down on her couch. Now what am I supposed to do? Maybe I should wake her. I watch television mindlessly. I'm annoyed. Once again, Annie has given me another useless day.

"Tonight at ten . . . There could be spyware on your computer. Find out how hackers gain access to your files without your knowledge."

I sit up a little straighter in my seat. That news clip just gave me an idea. I wonder if I can get into Annie's computer while she's asleep. I mean, she did promise me a review if I cleaned out my car. I'm sure she wouldn't mind if I helped myself while she napped. Annie begins to snore and I'm convinced she's in such a deep sleep it's definitely in my best interest to not wake her.

I tiptoe down the hall. I'm not sure why I'm being quiet all of the sudden. I probably could scream bloody murder and she wouldn't notice. But there's something about doing something you're not supposed to do that makes you think you need to be a quiet little mouse.

As soon as I get to her office, I peek around the corner one more time to see if she's coming before I slightly close the door. It takes me a few minutes to figure out how to turn on her computer. I've never actually used one this old before. I feel like it belongs in a museum.

It begins to churn and I'm reminded just how slow it is. Sitting there makes me feel nervous and now I have to pee. I squeeze my knees together tightly. There's no way I'm making any sounds to wake her.

Assuming she fell asleep right after we got home and she takes a daily two-hour nap, like yesterday, I should still have an hour.

Rolling my neck until it cracks, I realize how tense I am. I need to get better at this spy stuff. I stare at the blue screen as it continues its ridiculous process. Pushing up from the seat, I open the door slightly and listen for the wood cutter. Sure enough, she's still sawing away.

This is crazy. It has to have been like ten minutes and it's still loading. As I sit back down, my knee hits a drawer. "Fuck," I whisper as I rub it. I glance at it again. "Well, hello there. What secrets do you keep?"

It's not locked, but it's almost sealed shut. As I try to pull on it, I wonder if she's ever even used it. On my third try, it finally gives an inch. I yank it open and it squeaks. I cringe and pause to listen for footsteps. I breathe deeply when I still hear her snores.

There are a bunch of cards piled up inside and it smells musty and old. I call that smell "Eau de Annie." I chuckle to myself at the thought.

I grab a handful and start flipping through them.

"I used to think love was gift I'd never receive until the day you walked into my life. I didn't know a heart could feel so much so soon. My sun shines brighter, my grass looks greener, my sky is bright. You are the missing piece I never knew I needed. You've changed my world." I flip the card open. "I love you."

It's blank inside. No signature, just a plain card. It's beautiful, but damn. I was hoping someone actually gave it to her. I open another and another. All beautiful cards. Some almost bring a tear to my eye, but none of them have ever been used. I wonder if Annie is a romantic. Why would she have all these cards about love that she never sent?

The screen suddenly whirrs to life. I grab all the cards and quickly stuff them back in the drawer. Moving the mouse, a password box pops up. Shit. I tap my bottom lip. What would Annie use as a password? I type in Stupid. When that doesn't work I try Rhode. That was probably a dumb idea. I stare around the room, trying to think like Annie. I type hate. That doesn't work either. A warning message appears. Dammit! I quickly shut it down.

I thought that was my in. Now what am I going to do? I need to find Annie's password and soon. Something tells me it's the only way to get what I need. Annie is going down one way or another.

After the computer debacle I decide to continue snooping. Annie's still fast asleep, so I take my chances and sift through her mail in the kitchen. Every bill is opened and folded into a neat pile. Electricity, gas, insurance . . . boring. Then I see a bill for flowers. It's from a local place and she spent a chunk of change on them. Who in the hell is she sending flowers to and why would someone so in need of money waste so much on something so frivolous?

I flip to the next piece of mail. It's not opened yet. It's from a financial place. I wonder if it's a past due notice.

"What do you think you're doin'?"

Spinning quickly to the sound of her voice, I drop all her mail on the floor.

She sucks her bottom lip into her mouth and I feel

like I can see her heart pounding in her chest.

"I was . . ." Oh shit, think, Joss. "I was looking for the review you said you had for me."

"In my mail? You think I'm dumb? You were going through my things. See anything good?" She places her hands on her hips and I immediately feel like I got called to the principal's office for cheating. She stares from my eyes to the mail scattered on the floor.

I bend over to gather it and she shouts, "Don't touch it. That's mine."

She rushes over and starts picking up every piece and reorganizing it. My chest hurts. I feel awful.

She pauses at the bill for flowers and I hear her make that cracking noise in her mouth. "You need to go."

"Annie, I'm sorry. I was just bored. I shouldn't have touched your mail."

"I can't do this. Not today. You need to leave."

"But . . . I really didn't mean to upset you."

"I don't want you here. I don't want to do this anymore. You is a sneak and a liar. I don't like you. Now get outta my house!" Her voice shrills and I'm frightened. Taking a step back, I decide maybe I should leave before she kills me.

I rush toward the front door and grab my duffle bag. Panic sets in as I realize I may never get what I came here for. I turn to face her. "But what about the review you promised me?"

The responding look on her face causes me to bolt to my car. That was a really dumb move. I might have blown the whole thing.

# CHAPTER Eleven

ONCE I GET TO my car and hear her front door slam, I start to pace and pick at my nail polish. I really fucked up. I lean on my door and try to think. How can I make this right?

He clears his throat and that's when I realize I'm not alone.

His eyes travel from my incredibly short shorts to my pink flip-flops and then up to my worried expression. I like the way he's looking at me. Maybe I should wear my new shorts every day.

"Are you okay?"

I don't know why, but I rush to him. His arms encase me as I fly into them. He's dirty today. He must have been working outside. I don't care.

"Whoa! What's going on?" His hands frame my cheeks as he gently pulls me away to look into my eyes.

"I've had the worst day ever."

He doesn't say another word. He wraps his arms around me and pulls me close. His hand gently rubs my back. He's magical and just what I need. A hug from a man is way different than a sister or friend hug. There's something about strong arms around you that makes the world seem safer. There's something about *these* arms that are better than anything else in the world right now.

When I remember we literally just met and I'm about to uncharacteristically dry hump his leg, I pull away. I suddenly feel awkward about the whole thing. "I'm sorry."

"For what?" he asks as I take a step back.

"For charging you like that. We barely know each other."

"I actually thought it was perfect. You felt good up against me."

My eyes light up and I grin. "You know, I thought you were shy, but you're not. Are you?"

His head teeters. "I may be a bit shy at times." He pinches his fingers together briefly. "But I'll tell you what. When a hot girl jumps into my arms, I know well enough to let her stay there as long as she wants."

Why is he so cute and perfect? Even with his cap on backward and his sweaty shirt and filthy clothes, I'd still eat him alive. What's wrong with me? Maybe it's been too long. "You think I'm hot?" I ask, my smile returning.

He shakes his head. "Nice shorts."

"Annie made them for me. Annie . . ." I gaze around Rhode and back at her house to look for her.

"Do you want to tell me what happened? You sounded frantic earlier and never called me back. I was worried about you. Then I get home and see you wearing a path in the street. Something big must have gone down. What's got you so upset?"

I close my eyes and shake my head. "It's been a ridiculous day."

He gazes into my eyes, then down at his clothes. "I'm a mess." Turning his head to his house, he says, "Would you like to come inside?"

"Really?" Forgetting about Annie for a while is just what I need.

His white teeth shine out on his dirty face. "I asked, didn't I?"

"All right, but I'm going to move my car in front of your house, if that's okay. I'm fairly certain Annie already called the police on me."

"Now I really want to know what's going on. I'll leave the front door unlocked. Come inside when you're finished. I need to clean up a bit."

As he walks back to his house, I can't help but watch him. How is this man single?

After I move my car, fluff my hair, and chew a piece of gum, I open his front door.

The second I enter, I find myself smiling from ear to ear. There are stacks of old vinyl records in the corner of his living room and a turntable on top of an odd looking stand with two gigantic speakers and some kind of receiver. I'm pretty sure my grandparents used to have something like it when I was younger. A dark brown leather chair faces it and I can picture him sitting there listening to music. An old guitar is propped up in the opposite corner. I wonder if he plays.

Walking toward the records, I lean forward, curious to see what kind of music he likes. I see Bob Dylan, The Doors, Chicago, and Bon Jovi. He must like the classics. It fits him. He seems like an old soul.

As much as I'd like to bend down and look through them, I decide against it. My nosiness already pissed off Annie. I don't want to alienate Rhode too.

His house is different from Annie's. It's not only the layout, but also his style. He's old school with modern flare. I don't know how else to describe it, but I like it. I like him.

After a few minutes, a freshly showered Rhode turns the corner. He's wearing a white T-shirt and faded jeans that sit on his waist like they were made for him. His hair is wet and he's drying it with a towel.

"Sorry about that. Can I get you something to drink?"

"What do you have?"

He motions with his head for me to follow him, so I do. Tossing the towel on a chair, he opens the fridge. He leans down to look inside. "I have beer, beer, and beer. Any of those sound good?"

"Hmm . . ." I place my finger on my lips like I'm thinking. "I'll take a beer."

He smiles, pops the cap, and hands me a bottle. I take a really long drink. He seems entertained.

He points to his left to a room off the kitchen with a large TV and a couple of couches. "Want to sit down?"

I nod. I remove my flip-flops and curl my legs under myself. He clears his throat in what almost sounds like a moan.

He sits on the opposite couch. He's really far away.

"Do you play guitar?"

"I strum chords and pretend I play," he says with a smile.

"So you're a vinyl man?"

"I like the way it sounds. There's something about the static of the needle hitting a record that I find exciting."

I nod. "I'm a CD girl myself."

He smirks and I feel a little weird.

"I like your house. Thanks for inviting me inside."

"Do you live around here?" he asks, bringing the bottle to his lips.

"About twenty-five minutes, give or take traffic. I can't afford a house yet. Maybe I should have gone into landscaping. Only problem is I don't look good dirty."

"I highly doubt that's true. Something tells me you'd look amazing sweaty and covered in mud."

His eyes meet mine and he doesn't look away.

Raising my eyebrows at him, I smile. "Think maybe your boss would hire me?"

"He might. You might have to get on your hands and knees and show him what you can do first. With weeds I mean." He winks at me and snickers.

"Oh my God." I laugh. "Show me to your boss then."

"Yeah, about that. It mind kind of be me."

I smile. "I know."

"You do?" he questions as his head turns to the side to regard me.

"I might have done a little research. I like to know who I'm dealing with."

"Should I be flattered or worried?" He laughs.

"It's part of what I do. I'm actually working as a fact-checker right now. I basically make sure the information we're provided has credible sources. But this story could be my break. I guess you knew that from the run in with my mom the other day. I never did get to apologize."

"For what?"

I take another sip of my beer. "Oh jeez, I don't know. Her comment about my assignment being you or when she called you a sex-object. Maybe my comment about shagging you on my sister's table?"

He grins. "Oh, that."

"I'm surprised you didn't run away."

"Nah. It happens all the time."

I smile brightly and he licks his lips.

"Well my family is a little odd, but I guess you're used to odd since you live next to Annie." As soon as I say her name I feel ill. He must see it on my face because his gaze becomes probing.

"Do you want to talk about it?" he asks in a soothing tone.

"I feel like I talk too much. And complain *way* too much. I'd like to forget today. Tell me something. Distract me."

He leans forward, resting his elbows on his knees before taking a sip of his beer. He leans back on the couch and crosses his leg. His eyes seem to scan my body and it sets me on fire. "Distract you, huh?" He scratches his face, then places his beer on a side table. "Come with me."

He takes my beer and puts it next to his. He holds out his hand and I place mine inside. He's smoldering right now and my skin is on fire. Oh, shit. Is he taking me to bed?

"Does this involve me having to get on my hands

and knees?" I ask with a seductive smile.

He gazes down into my eyes. "Only if you want to."

The way he stares at me makes me tighten my thighs. I suddenly realize I forgot to pee. "Do you mind if I use your bathroom first?"

"Sure. Down the hall to the left."

Once I'm inside, I immediately start cleaning myself up. Thank God I shaved today. I wad up some toilet paper and start cleaning my girly parts. Shit, I hope I smell okay. I sniff my armpits. I open his bathroom cabinet to see what I can use to freshen up. I spit my gum into a tissue and use a little of his toothpaste on my teeth. I'm taking too long.

I stare at myself in the mirror. *Kitty, you're about to get pet*. I'm nervous and excited all at once.

I open the door and lean seductively on the frame. He's nowhere in sight.

"Rhode?" I holler in my most alluring voice.

"Over here."

Turning the corner, I see he's on his back patio. Are we fucking outside? He *is* an outdoor man.

"So you wanted me to distract you, right?" he asks.

"Yes . . . distract me," I say in a hot whisper as I step outside.

He does a double take at me. "Hey, you've got a little something blue on your teeth."

"What?"

He moves toward me. "Hold still." He lifts his finger and scrapes something off my tooth. I blink rapidly and place my teeth together awkwardly. Did that just happen?

"There you go." He wipes his hand on his jeans and turns away like it was nothing. "This is my garden."

My legs won't move. He thought he'd distract me by showing me his garden? What the fuck? I thought I'd see a hose, but this isn't what I had in mind.

"Over here are my tomato plants, then cucumbers, carrots, spinach, corn, and potatoes. You can't beat fresh vegetables and nothing gets my mind off things like getting down and gardening."

Rubbing my arms, I try to smile. He wanted to show me his veggie garden? On my hands and knees? That's really . . . sweet. I wonder how big his cucumbers are. I could use something sizeable right now. Damn, I had him all wrong. I swore he was propositioning me. At minimum, checking me out.

He's so proud of himself and I'm doing my best to stop thinking of sex. "I like to try out new stuff. It's one of the reasons poor Annie is always my guinea pig for dinner."

"I like to try new stuff, too," I say hesitantly as my mind wanders. What I'd like to try is screwing Rhode in the garden. Maybe him pounding me from behind on his kitchen table. Straddling him on his leather chair. Showing me his carrot stick…

He waves his hand in front of my face. "Where did you go just now?"

Shaking my head, I smile widely. "Umm, I was thinking you never really told me about how you became friends with Annie." Good. Change the subject.

"That's a long story. How much time do you have?" He laughs.

"Well, considering I don't think she'll ever talk to

me again, I have the rest of the week."

"Will you please tell me what happened?"

I sigh. "I looked at her mail while she was sleeping. I was bored and curious."

He cringes. "Rule number one with Annie is don't invade her privacy."

I slouch and put my hands on my hips. "That would have been nice to know YESTERDAY!"

He smirks and I stare at his mouth a little too long. He steps toward me and brushes a strand of hair from my eyes. I gaze up into his. Is this it? Is he going to kiss me?

I lean slightly toward him, licking my lips. He takes a step back and stares at me like kissing me was the last thing he was thinking. I can no longer meet his gaze. Wrong again. How embarrassing.

"Umm . . . Can I tell you why I called you earlier?" he asks.

"I should go." I pivot on my heel and rush toward the door. I pull it, then push it. It won't open.

He stands next to me at the door while I place my forehead against it. "Are you going to let me explain?"

"No."

"Should I not have touched your hair?" he asks.

I snicker. "You should have touched a lot more. Oh yeah, Joss. You'd look hot dirty. Get on your hands and knees, Joss," I say in a mocking tone. "Fucking ridiculous! Then you back away from me? Now open the door, please, so me and what's left of my pride can go."

"Please wait. Let me talk to you for a minute."

"The time for talking has come and gone. I need to get out of here."

"But I really want to explain."

"Open the door. Open the door. Open the door!" I shout it each time with increasing volume, stomping my foot for extra emphasis.

He pushes it in then pulls it open. "It's tricky."

Pulling my keys from my shorts, I jog to my car. "Yeah. It's tricky, all right."

"Come on! Don't go like this. You're barefoot! What about your shoes?" he yells, as he follows me out the door. His hands fly to the top of his head.

"Throw them away. They aren't worth another second with you."

His reaction to my words causes me physical pain. Maybe now he knows how rejection feels.

I jump in my car and drive barefoot all the way home. I'm a fucking idiot. I will never ever like another man for as long as I live. And never, ever . . . Rhode Bennett.

# Chapter Twelve

**IT'S A LITTLE AFTER** ten and I've eaten an entire pint of cookie dough ice cream, another can of barbeque Pringles, and a half a slice of cheese. I'm going to turn into a blimp if I keep eating my emotions. This whole thing with Annie has me so upset. The thing with Rhode didn't help either. Maybe I over reacted. I was already on edge from my argument with Annie and he just seemed to push all my buttons.

I think about it for a minute. No. He was flirty and sexy and then acted like I was crazy for trying to kiss him. Fuck that. I was right to be pissed.

On the other hand, I feel awful for betraying Annie's trust the way I did. Even though my plan is still to expose her, I want to expose her because she gives me what I need, not because I steal it. Would Darla be disappointed in me for snooping? I could go to work tomorrow and tell them I'm back from vacation. I'd have to explain that the story didn't work out and leave Darla alone for three months. I'm guessing she'd probably never look at me the same way again. She'd know I gave up. Or failed. I'm not sure which is worse.

Or I could beg Annie for another chance. Jumping up from my seat, a burst of adrenaline surges through me. It could be a sugar high, but I'm going with it. Dressed in my sweats and a T-shirt, I slide on my flats and grab my keys. I'll make this right one way or another.

"Annie, please let me in. I know it's late, but I can't stand how we left things."

I bang on her door and ring her doorbell over and over again. The dog barking is loud and obnoxious. She has to hear me, assuming she's home. After my fourth and final attempt, I decide to try again in the morning. I'll have to think of something better to say. As the barking door chime comes to an end, I take two steps off her porch.

A clicking bolt and a loud squeak catches my attention. "Who let the dogs out?" she sings before barking and dancing around.

My mouth hits the floor.

"You know that song?" she asks, laughing. "Woof, woof, woof, woof, woof!"

She pushes on the door hard to open it fully, almost stumbling out the door with a bottle of Scotch clutched in her hand.

"Annie? Are you okay?"

"Child, I'm divine." She takes a swig out of her bottle and waves me to follow her as she goes back inside.

"What the ever loving fuck?" I mumble as I enter.

Annie laughs as she trips over nothing. She takes another sip from her bottle. It's half empty. "Damn cat," she says, looking from left to right as if she tripped over him. I glance around and Stupid is curled up in a ball on a chair in the corner.

"Have you been drinking?" I ask, shocked.

"Oh, child, you is smart! What gave it away? The fact I'm holding a bottle of booze or that I drank it in front of you?"

I guess I was stating the obvious. I'm just surprised. Maybe I should be happy drunk Annie let me in the house. Never mind she's still mean. "Is this what you do at night?"

"No, just tonight."

My gut churns. "I'm sorry, Annie. I didn't mean to upset you. I feel awful that I made you drink."

"You?" She laughs. "You think this is because of you?" She shakes her head and takes another drink before looking at the ceiling. "You hear that, Bobby? She thinks I give a shit!"

"Bobby?" I question.

"Jossssillynn," she begins, slurring my name, "this is Bobby!"

There's clearly no one in the room and now I'm feeling concerned for her sanity. "Annie, maybe you should sit down."

I reach out for her right before she sits backward into a chair that isn't there. She falls backward on the floor and begins to laugh. She never spills a drop of Scotch.

"Holy shit!" I bend down to help her up.

"You said sit. You trying to kill me?"

I help her onto the couch and she takes another drink.

"Annie, can I have that bottle?"

She clutches it to her chest. "Get your own!"

"I don't want to drink it. I think maybe you've had enough for tonight."

She stares into my eyes and then looks at the bottle briefly before handing it to me. "Yeah, I guess I did enough remembering. It tastes like piss anyway. I don't know why he liked it so much."

"Who?" I take the bottle from her hands.

"Bobby. He lovvvved his Scotch. He used to have a drink every night after we left work. He said it's what helped him be so romantic. I think he was born that way. You can try to teach a man how to treat a lady, but sometimes, that shit is genetic. His daddy was a charmer and, boy oh boy, did Bobby know how to woo me." She smiles brightly.

I sit down on the floor next to her and crisscross my legs.

"You and he dated?"

"Oh, we did more than date. We worked together writing greeting cards. People used to say Bobby and I were magic. I can tell you this. I felt magic in my crotch every time he looked at me."

I wince just a little before turning away to smile. She's something else. "You worked at a greeting card company?" I guess that explains the cards I found in her desk drawer. She's a wealth of information tonight.

"Yessiree, Bob. I was a poet and Bobby was my muse. He said I was his too. We used to sit on his front porch and sip lemonade at night comin' up with ideas for cards. Boss loved us. He said we were the money. Ah, those were the days."

Her smile slowly fades. She takes the bottle of Scotch out of my hand, takes one more swig, and then gives it back to me.

"We dated for years. Snuck a kiss here and there. Maybe even touched a little. Things were different back then. We didn't go flaunting our titties and screwing everything in sight. Sex was for marriage. We shoulda waited."

"You didn't?" I ask, almost excited to hear something about her life.

"Bobby had a bulge in his pants for me." She grabs at her crotch. "You know how you can sometimes see it when a man moves? How you watch for a glimpse of it? Well, Bobby had a ding dong dinner that was fit for a deep love channel."

I chuckle.

"His pecker was long and thick. Oh, oh, oh . . . I knew it was gonna be a mind-blowin' orgasm. Now it's not like I hadn't fingered myself, but a dick does the trick. Know what I mean?" she asks as she elbows me.

"Yeah. Thanks for the visual." I cringe.

"But ooh, I wanted that hard rocket in my space museum."

I snort.

"When he asked me to marry him, I was ready to give it all away."

My eyes open wide. "Marry him?"

She smiles and leans forward. "He asked my daddy and everything. My daddy was a hard man. He didn't show emotion. But Bobby told me he thought he was gonna cry when Bobby asked for my hand. My daddy loved me even though he ain't never said it. He didn't have to. I knew."

She stares off into the distance and I think about my own father for a moment. I love him to pieces. He's quiet too, but that's mostly because my mom never lets him speak.

"Bobby told me he had a card he was working on and wanted my thoughts. He asked me to read it out loud. It was beautiful. It was all the things a girl wants to hear a man say. How she makes it hard for him to breathe. How he can't stop looking at her. How she's the first thing he thinks of when he wakes up and his last thought before he closes his eyes. How she makes him feel like he could take on the world as long as she was by his side. It was lovely. When I moved the card he was on one knee. He said the words back to me and asked me if I'd be his."

My heart flutters in my chest. I wonder what that kind of love must feel like.

"So what happened?"

"I fucked him, that's what happened."

"That night?" My eyes bulge anew.

"No . . . right before the wedding. The night before. I couldn't wait for that chunk of a man."

"Okay . . ."

"Oh, child, it was more than okay. That man's cock was a rooster. I made him cock a doodle do like he was high on feed and the sun was just startin' to rise!"

"Again . . . thanks for the visual," I say with a laugh.

"He sucked and bucked me like I was a doe and he had a game record to break."

She's quiet for a while after that. She shakes her head. "Well, time for bed." She tries to stand and falls back into the couch. "Maybe I should sleep here."

She curls into a ball. I pull the blanket from behind her and cover her.

"Annie?"

"What?" she whispers as she closes her eyes.

"What happened to Bobby?"

"I told you. I fucked him."

I snicker. "Yeah, I got that. But how did he . . . die? He is dead, right?"

Her eye cracks open. "My pooty is strong. It's a weapon. I gave that man a heart attack. Now I make sure to only screw men who're younger than me." She smiles and closes her eyes. "Night, Bobby. Happy woulda been anniversary."

I kneel down next to her and stare at Angry Annie. It's the most she's ever told me. I should have asked about reviews while she was so talkative. Staring down at the bottle, I take a swig and toast the sky. The pieces of Annie are starting to fall into place.

# CHAPTER Thirteen

I HAVE TO DROP off some papers for Claus at work before I go to Annie's and since I have some extra time, I decide to make a cupcake run. I half-considered getting something greasy for Annie since I'm sure she has a hangover, but I feel like cake today. Maybe my sister's cake can convince her that the bakery is amazing. Jorgie makes the very best of everything.

The bakery isn't open yet, but I'm hoping she'll see me and let me in before everyone else. I lean my head against the glass to look inside. The lights are off in the main room, but a glow from the back tells me she's there, as usual.

I'm just about to tap on the glass, when she walks out from the store room. I wave my hands in the air around my head, but she doesn't see me. She's smiling brightly and glancing over her shoulder. She says something and laughs.

I follow her line of vision and stop breathing when I see Rhode walking behind her. He says something in response to her and smiles. She walks over to him and places her hand on his arm. He wraps his hand over hers. It's intimate and alarming all at once.

The way he's looking at her makes my heart sink. He pulls her into a hug. I know how those feel. I turn away from the window and lean my back against the brick wall. I can't bear to watch them kiss. Forcing back the tears that threaten my eyes, I try to understand why he's here and what he's doing with her.

Of course! It's Jorgie. That's why he pulled away! He's seeing my sister. It all makes sense.

I saw their connection when they first met. Jorgie is sweet and kind. Rhode is shy and hot. The hot guy always gets the good girl. But the things he said to me? Did I misunderstand everything? Was it about gardening the whole time?

I squeeze my eyes closed tightly and take a deep breath. Why I'm reacting this way? I guess sometimes you don't realize how much you want a person until they're no longer a possibility. By the way my chest aches, I can tell I must have really wanted him. More than I've wanted someone in a long time. I thought maybe there were sparks between us, but I thought wrong. He's with my sister. I'd never ever stand in the way of Jorgie's happiness. If she wants him then she gets him. End of story. I hurry to my car and pull away before anyone can see me. The last thing I want is to look like I was watching them.

After I drop off my paperwork, I grab a big bag of McDonald's breakfast foods. I'm going to eat until my pants burst. Good thing I wore yoga pants today. At the rate I'm going, this article is going to turn me into a whale. I vow to go for a run tonight. I need to sweat out all of my feelings. Plus, when you're sweating, no one can see when you're really crying. I barely knew him. It's no big deal. Right?

I knock on Annie's door and no surprise, she doesn't answer. I try the door and it's open. "Annie? I'm coming in, don't shoot me!"

When I drop the bag in front of her at the kitchen table she gazes up at me as if I did something wrong.

"What are you doing here? I told you to get out and I meant it."

"But, I thought after last night—"

"Last night? Whatchoo talkin' 'bout?"

I slide into the seat at her table and open the bag. "You don't remember?"

"Did we have a date? 'Cause I remember having a date with my man Scotch, but not you."

"Oh, you and Scotch had a party last night for sure!" I laugh as I remove a sandwich from the bag.

She stares me down, making my smile slowly slide away. My mouth falls open when she says nothing.

"How about this?" I ask, singing "Who Let the Dogs Out" to see if it jogs her memory.

She cringes. "What's the matter with you? You crazy? You hit your head this morning? Comin' in here and singing some dumbass song actin' like we're friends. Bringin' me hash browns like it's a peace offering and I'm a NATO officer," she mumbles under her breath.

"I came over last night and apologized. You were drunk. We bonded."

"I don't get drunk and the only thing I bond with is my dentures."

This day hasn't gone the way I planned. "I'm so

confused," I say, placing my hands on the table.

"You forgot dumb. You dumb too."

Her comment is the straw that broke the camel's back. I slump down into my chair and place my head in my hands. The damn breaks and I start to cry. "I'm so tired and sad and tired and so, so sad."

"What the biscuit mix?" she says as I sob.

She grabs the stack of napkins and tosses them at me. "You gonna make your hussy makeup run. Stop it!"

"I can't stop. This whole day—the whole week . . . Actually, it's my life in general. I don't want to be a fact-checker anymore. I want to be more than that, you know?" My tears flow down my cheeks.

Annie's brows furrow as I continue to spill my thoughts along with my tears.

"I practically threw myself at him, and he likes my sister. Of course he does. Everyone loves Jorgie. She's smart and kind and beautiful and good. She's a good person and he's a good person. I'm not . . . good." My eyes dart to Annie's face and it's sullen.

"I shouldn't have snooped through your things. I'm so sorry, but you said you'd tell me about your reviews and I cleaned my car and you were sleeping and I was bored. And I suck. I've eaten ice cream, and chips, and now McDonald's."

I take a big bite of my McGriddle sandwich and talk with food in my mouth. "And you know what? I don't even care. What's the point of being skinny if the guy you like likes someone else? Huh? What's the point?"

I stuff another bite into my already full mouth and

sob as I chew. Annie stares at me and crosses her arms.

"You need a therapist, child. You got something wrong with you up here," she says, pointing to her head.

I cry harder.

"Oh, for the sake of Peter, Paul, and Mary. You need to stop your whining. You want something, you gotta make it happen. You want a man, go get him. Don't let some other woman steal what's yours."

"But it's Jorgie. I love her."

"But you want his tickler. I assume we're talkin' about lawnmower boy next door."

"No!" I sniffle nervously. Shit. She's going to say something. "It's not him. It's someone else."

She stands and walks to the sink. "You're the worst liar I ever seen."

"What's a tickler?"

"A dick."

"Is everything about sex with you?"

"When you get to be my age there are some things you remember more fondly than others. I know the look on your face. It screams 'Cut my grass!'"

"Forget I said anything. It's not him, okay? Just drop it."

"Mm hmm."

"Annie, please!" I say, hurrying to face her.

She rolls her eyes. "Understand this . . . I don't care who you're crying over or why you're sad. All I'm saying is stop."

"Fine. I'm done. No more tears." I wipe my cheeks with my hands and scrub my nose. Standing next to her, I notice she's placed her cup of coffee in the sink.

There's another one on the table. I glance between them. "Did you pour me coffee?" I ask, rubbing my nose once more.

"Nope."

"Then why are there two cups?"

"I'm havin' another."

"Why would you use another mug?"

"'Cause I felt bad that one hadn't been used in a while."

Picking up the cup, I notice it has cream and smells like vanilla. I stare at the cup until it hits me. She acted like I was coming to protect herself, but she was waiting for me. Prickly Annie strikes again. I smile brightly and sniff away my tears.

"Nu-uh . . . Don't you go thinking I poured that for you." She takes the cup from my hands and walks toward the sink.

"Wait! Can I have it? Please?"

She sighs. "It's probably cold now. I don't want it anymore. No sense wasting it." She places it in front of me and I take a sip. It is cold, but I drink it anyway. I'd never complain about her being nice. Assuming she knows how. Maybe I'm growing on her.

"You do remember my being here last night, don't you?"

"Nope."

"Do you remember telling me about Bobby and your greeting cards?" I ask.

"Who's Bobby?"

"Oh, come on, Annie. It's the most you've told me since I met you. I wish you'd drink all the time. Is that why you were so angry with me yesterday? Was it just a bad day?"

"You were goin' through my things! Would you like that?"

"No," I say, lowering my head.

"And then I knew you saw the flower bill."

I shrug.

"That was none of your business," she says angrily.

"You're absolutely right."

There's a moment of silence before she speaks again. "I send flowers to Bobby's grave once a year."

I nod and I can tell she's getting upset. I decide to change the subject.

"Hey, do you want to see my car now?"

"Why would I want to see that hunk of junk?"

"You told me yesterday that if I cleaned it, you'd give me a review. I'm still waiting."

"Speaking of which." She holds out her hand and I know what she wants.

I pull the money out of my purse and place it in her palm. I watch her count it and hold the bills up to the light again. It seems to be her thing.

"How many reviews do you need to be outta my hair?" She does that clicking thing with her teeth again as she stares at me.

I lick my lips. "Three? Four tops. And I need to know why you write them. Honestly . . . why do you write what you do?"

The theme song for "Cops" sounds on my phone. I glance down at it, reject the call, and push it away from me.

"You wanted or something'?"

"Just by one cop in particular."

"What did you do?"

"Not what you think. I promised him a date if he helped me with a lead. He calls every day. Anyway, as I was saying, how do you decide what you're going to review and where to post it?"

"And?" she questions, crossing her arms.

"And what?"

"Are you going to go out with him?"

"No, I'm not. He's nice enough, but there will never be anything between us. He's not my type."

"Does he know that?"

I wrinkle my nose.

"You gotta tell him you got heat in your pants for lawnmower boy."

"Heat in my pants? There's zero heat here." I make an X over me with my hands. "I told you, Rhode isn't the guy I was talking about."

"Uh-huh. 'Cause you got so many options and they just chasin' you around town."

A breeze flows through my hair and I remember Annie's kitchen windows are open. Worry tugs at my mind. I stand and nonchalantly glance out the back window. The last thing I want is Rhode to be outside and have heard any of this conversation. Not seeing anyone, I quickly turn to face her, speaking more quietly than before, just in case. "How would you know what my options are? There are plenty of men I can date."

"Name one. The Po-Po doesn't count."

I struggle to think of a single person because they don't exist. I blurt out random males I know. "There's Steve from accounting, George who works at a restaurant, and Tom who I met at a bar." There's no reason to tell her Steve is my grandfather's age, George is my regular pizza delivery guy, and Tom is my sister's ex, who I did actually happen to meet at a bar.

"Call one of them. Ask them out."

"I don't want to. I don't have time for relationships. How did we end up talking about me? Let's get back to reviews."

"We can't talk about reviews because you're pining to have your garden seeded."

"Where do you come up with this shit?" I ask her. "I don't need my garden raked, seeded, or picked. My garden is just fine. If I wanted to, I could go out with anyone."

"Prove it. For all I know, this cop is calling 'cause you're wanted for stealing people's mail."

I roll my eyes at her. "I told you, he wants a date."

"Sure he does. He wants a date with a judge because you stole shit."

"Dammit, Annie. I swear he wants to go out with me. Now drop it."

She shrugs and takes a hash brown from the bag. Sitting at the table, she starts to eat it, shaking her head and tsking me.

"What? What now?" I ask, irritated.

"I feels sorry for you. It must hurt that you can't get a date. I know when I was your age I was busy all the time. I guess no one wants to hang out with your sorry little ass."

"For fuck's sake! You want proof? Fine! Listen to this."

I dial Adam's number on speakerphone and he

picks up almost immediately. "Hey, Adam, it's Joss. Did you call?"

"Hey there, beautiful!"

I stick my tongue out at Annie and she huffs.

Adam continues, "I called you because I was wondering if you're ready for that date you promised me?"

"The date *you* wanted? With me?" I point to the phone smugly. "Sure. How about tonight?"

"That would be fantastic. I'll pick you up at seven. We can try that new Italian place on 42nd Street. I think it's called Zoro's."

"You know what? I'm going to be working late, so I'll just meet you there."

"Joss, I want a full service date, remember? That was the deal. That means I get to pick you up and drop you off."

Ugh. I hate this whole thing. "Fine, but when you say full service that means a car ride and dinner. Nothing more."

"I know that!" He laughs. "No need to worry. You're safe with me, sweetheart. I'll see you tonight."

"Wait! Do you need to know where I live?"

"Nope, I have it covered."

I was right. He did check up on me. Yuck.

"Hey, how did that address I gave you check out?" he asks.

"Okay, gotta go. See you tonight. Bye." I end the call quickly before he has the chance to mention Annie. That's the last thing I need right now. "Happy?" I ask, cocking my head to the side.

"A big person can admit when they're wrong." She shoves the last of her hash brown in her mouth and chews.

"Yes, they can." I stare at her while she finishes, waiting for an apology.

"What? You got a chewing fetish?"

"I'm waiting."

"For what?"

"For you to admit that you were wrong."

"Why would I do that? I'm not wrong."

Leaning forward on the table, I grab a hold of my roots with my hands. This woman is so frustrating. I take a deep breath. "Can we get back to how you review now? I've been here for three days and I still know nothing."

"You're right. You don't know anything."

I know she wants to upset me, but I'm not going to let her change the subject again. "What about this?" I ask, lifting the bag of McDonald's. "Would this be something you'd review after eating it?"

"No."

"How about the Scotch from last night?"

"Nope."

"Why not?" I question.

"Because I got nothin' to say about it."

"What makes you want to write a review then?"

She wipes her fingers on a napkin, stands, and walks into the living room, turning on the TV.

Hoping she's going to show me something, I follow her.

She's flipping channels. She skips over the shows and stops when a commercial comes on. "Like this," she says, motioning to the TV with the remote in her hand. "This commercial plays fifty times a day, over and over and over again."

I listen intently to the ad.

"Do you hear that dumbass music?" she asks.

"Yes."

"Now why do they have to play it every single time the show goes to commercial? I've seen it so many times it makes me mad. If I had wanted a sweeper boot and ordered it for some reason, I would've changed my mind by now and cancelled my order."

"Did you write a review for the product?"

"Not yet."

"Are you going to?" I can't help but feel excited.

"I don't know."

"But that's how you decide what to write about? Annoying commercials?"

"Not always." She suddenly jerks her wrist. "Ooh, I got to go! I'm late."

"Go where?"

"It's Wednesday."

I'm not sure why she thinks I know what that means. "Annie, please. We were finally getting somewhere. Can you give me one review today? Just one? Please?"

"I'll give you one. But first we go do my errands." She turns off the TV and points to a bag by the front door. "You get the bag, I'll get the car."

"You're driving? No, no way!"

"Shut your mouth. You've been whining all day."

"You drive like a crazy woman."

"If a woman is crazy it's because some man made her that way."

I teeter my head back and forth because that's probably accurate. I lift the bag of what seems to be clothes and follow her out the back door. "Can you at least tell me where we're going?"

"You'll see when we get there."

I immediately buckle my seat belt and brace myself for impact. Annie slowly backs out of the driveway and carefully places the gear in drive. My head flips to regard her.

"It was a good show, huh?" she asks.

"You're not really an awful driver?" I question.

"I ever tell you my daddy was a stunt man?"

This woman . . . she's full of surprises. Hopefully she's also full of reviews.

# CHAPTER Fourteen

SLIDING MY FINGER ALONG the dew of my glass, I can't help but smile. I finally have a review. After a trip to the grocery store and another visit to Thea's house, Annie delivered as promised. My article has a starting point. Annie's mind is twisted, and it's a review, but I really need to get more dirt on her if this article is going to blow Darla's mind the way I want it to. It can't all be about TV commercials. My sister isn't advertised on TV. How did Jorgie's bakery upset her enough to warrant a review?

I decide to leave that worry for tomorrow. Tonight, I'm celebrating my small accomplishment. At least I'm making progress. I have two more days to get all the dirt and then I can be on my way.

"I hope I put that smile on your face," Adam asks, as he returns to his seat after a quick bathroom trip.

"In a roundabout way, you sort of did." Taking a large gulp of wine, I empty my glass. Liquor is all that's keeping me sane right now on this ridiculous date. Why did I let Annie talk me into this?

"Whoa! Either you're really thirsty or you're trying to get drunk."

I smile awkwardly and lie through my teeth. "It's good wine."

He reaches across the table to the bottle and pours me another glass. I motion for him to keep filling when he tries to stop halfway. I'd drink rubbing alcohol at this point.

Turning my head slightly over my shoulder, I try to make eye contact with the waiter. We've been waiting for our food for what seems like forever. I guess I could have another piece of bread, but I think I've had enough carbs for the night.

The place is packed for a Wednesday night. Adam tried to pull the cop card to get us a good table, but we had to take the one right near the entrance. It's fine by me. The entrance is also the exit. I like being near an out in case I have to make a run for it. I may have to run soon, especially if he licks his lips and looks at my mouth one more time.

"You look really nice tonight."

"Thanks."

"Did you ever find that lady you were looking for?" Adam pretends to scoot his chair closer to the table, but all he does is move closer to me.

"Yes, I did. Thanks again. It was really nice of you to help me."

He places his hand over mine and I pull it away and pretend to itch my head. Ugh. Can this night get any worse? I take another sip of my wine. I'd better slow down or I'm going to say something I'll regret.

"Hi, you should have an order under Rhode Bennett. I paid by credit card."

The sound of his voice makes me gasp and I start choking on my wine.

"Joss, are you okay?" Adam pats me on the back as I hack and wheeze.

I pray he didn't hear him say my name.

"Joss? Is that you?"

Dammit! I cough a bit more and cover my mouth with my napkin as Rhode walks over to the table. I can't breathe. It definitely went down the wrong pipe.

"Are you okay?" he asks.

"She's fine," Adam responds protectively. "And you are?"

Rhode watches me for a moment and then holds out his hand to Adam. "Rhode Bennett."

"Adam Donovan, police officer and Joss's date."

I clear my throat and simultaneously roll my eyes at Adam.

"How do you know my girl?" Adam asks.

His audacity makes me feel the need to speak. I barely make the words out through the burn.

"I'm no one's girl."

Rhode smirks at me briefly before returning his attention to Adam. "I live next door to Joss's friend, Annie."

"Annie McClintonuck?" Adam asks, leaning forward.

"That's right. Do you know her?"

"What are you doing here, Rhode?" I ask somewhat coherently, trying to divert the conversation before Adam gives me away.

"Annie asked me to get dinner from here tonight. She never asks for anything, so I thought it must be special."

I narrow my eyes. That stinker. What is she doing? I remember our conversation. Is she trying to set Rhode and me up together? Why else would she send him here? Rhode keeps looking back and forth between me and Adam. Is it possible he could be jealous? It would serve him right. Hmm . . .

I lean into Adam and give him an adoring smile before turning my attention to Rhode. "Adam asked me to dinner tonight. Some people like me, I guess." I hope he gets my drift.

"I'm sure there are a lot of people who like you, Joss."

He's riding the waves I'm creating. Let's see where this goes. He shoots me a cocky grin and it pisses me off. He thinks he knows me. He doesn't know anything!

"I know there are!" I reply confidently. "Some people aren't afraid to say what they feel while others send mixed messages."

His lips purse and I know in my gut it's to keep from smiling. Asshole. But dammit, why does he have to look so good all the time? He's got the scruffy beard back that I adore and his smile makes me want to lick his teeth. I hate him for liking my sister. My sister . . . I'm reminded why there will never be anything between us.

"I saw you at the bakery yesterday morning. I hope you got what you were looking for."

His smile drops. "You saw me?"

"Yeah. I guess you like Jorgie's muffins. She was always a better cook than me."

"Who said I liked her muffins?" he asks.

Adam glances back and forth between us like he's watching a tennis match.

"I could see you liked her muffins by the way you hugged them."

"He hugged her muffins?" Adam asks, confused.

"Shh," I say, waving him off but never breaking eye contact with Rhode. "This doesn't concern you."

Rhode's eyes meet mine. "Why would you think my hugging her had anything to do with her muffins?"

"Please," I say, rolling my eyes. "I could see the way you were looking at her. And you know what? That's great. Jorgie is an amazing girl, but if you hurt her, I will personally kick your ass."

Rhode leans forward directly in front of me, placing his hands on the table and squaring his body with mine. "For a smart girl you sure don't have a clue, do you?"

"Hey . . ." Adam says defensively as he stands.

I push him down with my hand.

"I know what I saw."

"Do you? Have you spoken to your sister?"

"I don't need to," I say, throwing my napkin on the table and standing up from my chair.

Rhode takes a step toward me. "I think before you go making assumptions you should get your facts straight. I'm surprised for a fact-checker that you don't do a better job at that."

Those are fighting words. "Who do you think you are?" I ask as I take a step closer to him.

"I think I'm the guy you didn't let explain himself last night."

Adam seems angry. "What the fu—"

Rhode and I glare at him saying the exact same thing. "Shut up."

Adam stands and throws his napkin on the table. There's a lot of napkin throwing going on.

"You didn't need to explain. You made yourself perfectly clear!" I shout, placing my hands on my hips. I think I see a vein twitch in his neck. We're really close. He smells good.

"You don't know anything about what I was going to say."

"Um, Mr. Bennett? Your food is ready."

A young girl holds out a bag to him as if her arm is a fishing rod and the bag is at the end of the line. I guess we've made quite a scene.

Brushing my hands on my pants, I sit back down in my chair. "Have a nice night, Rhode. Tell Annie I said hey."

Rhode glances at Adam for a moment before staring at me. If he's expecting me to say another word to him, he's going to be standing there all night. He's currently invisible to me. He takes his food and stomps out the door. I inhale a large gulp of wine.

Clenching my teeth, I decide I hate him and never want to see his ugly, beautiful, nasty face again. I shouldn't be jealous, but I am. I love and hate my sister for being so perfect.

"What in the hell was that all about?" Adam asks.

My heart sinks. "Nothing. Nothing at all."

# CHAPTER Fifteen

"I CANNOT BELIEVE YOU did that!"

"All I did was set the scene. You played the role."

"Is that why you wanted me to go on a date? You wanted to send Rhode there?"

"It worked out, didn't it?" Annie responds. "I knew I was right. It is lawnmower boy you're crushing on."

I open my mouth to deny it, but I don't see the point. I'm interested in what she knows.

Stupid swirls around my legs and I scratch his back. He's the highlight of my visits to Annie these days. "How was Rhode last night when he brought dinner?"

"Very irritated. Not himself at all."

"Good." I smile. "At least something came from it."

"How was your copper?"

"Awful. After the scene with Rhode, I had to avoid his advances all night. I'm afraid the only one who ended up jealous was Adam."

Stupid darts off toward the living room and runs into the wall again. I cringe as he shakes his head and keeps walking. You'd think he'd know the house lay-out better by now.

"Did you talk to your sister?" Annie asks.

"No, and I'm not going to. As far as I'm concerned the whole thing is over."

"Child, anyone can see from your face it isn't over."

"Can we please stop discussing my lack of a love life and talk about reviews again? I'm only here today and tomorrow and I we've barely scratched the surface."

Annie holds out her hand. Some things never change.

After several minutes of scrutinizing the money quality she finally places the bills in her wallet. I'm ready to get cracking. I need something juicier.

"Besides irritating TV commercials, what are other things that move you?"

"You mean like move my bowels? I ain't constipated."

I frown at her. "You know what I mean."

"Do I?" she asks, drying a glass.

"I mean make you want to write to someone. And why are they always negative?"

"What you talkin' about? They aren't bad. They're honest. I swear, everybody wants a trophy for getting out of bed. I'm telling people what I think."

"Yeah, but the review for the boot said it was a piece of garbage. You didn't even try it. How do you know it's bad?"

She points her finger at me. "You forgot I said the commercial was bad too."

"Basket Case" from Green Day sounds on my

phone. It's my ringtone for my mother. I quickly reject the call and focus on Annie. "Ugh. Sorry. Go ahead," I say, motioning to her to speak.

"There are a lot of reasons I write what I do. You wouldn't understand."

"Try me."

Once again, "Basket Case" sounds off. I slide the button to vibrate. "You were saying?"

"You sure are popular lately. Do you need to get that?" she asks, pointing.

"No. It's only my mom."

"Child, you answer your momma right now."

"No, you don't understand. She's awful."

"Don't you talk about her that way!"

"Annie, you've never met her. Trust me when I say she makes you look easy."

My phone begins to vibrate again.

"Pick it up or we're done."

"Are you serious?"

She nods.

"Okay, you asked for it. Here we go again." I press speaker and say hello.

"Why do I have to call you three times before you answer your phone?"

"Hi, Mom. Nice to hear your voice, too."

"I asked you a question."

"I'm working."

"You mean you're pretending to work."

I roll my eyes at Annie.

"What's up?" I ask.

"Your father has to go out of town for work on your birthday next month, so I'm calling an impromptu dinner tonight at five."

"It's not until next month. Why would we get together tonight?"

"Your father and I have plans and this is all I have free."

Annie's eyes open wide.

"That's okay. I'm fine with no family function. No need for a birthday celebration."

"Well, I'm the one who suffered through nineteen hours of labor with you and if I want to have a dinner to remember what my body used to be like before you destroyed it then you're going to come. You owe me at least your presence for what you did to me."

"Remembering your figure sounds really special and everything, and I'm touched that you want me to share in your special day, but no."

I hear static and multiple voices talking in the background.

"Hi, Joss. Please?"

I sigh. "I see she's playing the Dad card. Well played, Mom, well played. Did she tell you to make me feel guilty?"

"Yes. Yes, she did. But the truth is, I'd hoped to see you and I feel terrible about being out of town. So what do you say?"

"Can't you and I go to lunch another day?"

"We already spoke to Jorgie. Grandpa's already here and I know he wants to see you."

"Like I told Mom, I'm working. I can't."

"She ain't working," Annie says as she bends to look out the window.

"Really?" I question sarcastically, covering the

phone.

"You're just sitting there whining as usual."

"What was that? I couldn't hear," he asks.

Annie makes that clicking noise with her mouth and it gives me an idea. "Hey, Dad, is it okay if I bring someone?"

"Sure. Anyone special?"

"Oh, just my friend, Annie."

"Nu-uh. I ain't going," she says, leaning to speak into the phone.

"What? Who was that?"

"Don't worry. We'll see you later, Dad. Bye."

I quickly end the call and smile at Annie.

"You aren't dragging me to some family thing and I ain't your friend."

"You're the one who wanted me to call my mom. It's the least you can do for putting me in that situation."

"I don't owe you anything."

"The hell you don't! I've given you four hundred and twenty dollars for one review, some ruined jeans, and a lot of grief. Today, you are going to give me another review and then you're coming to my mom's stupid pretend party for me."

"You think you gonna tell me what to do?"

"Yes. Yes, I do."

"Humph."

I sigh. She's so stubborn. "Please? You made me take the call. I already said you were coming and I could use a buffer with my mom. Then she can see that I am trying to do an article. You can talk about your review process."

"I thought you said it was dinner, not a symposium."

"You heard my mom . . . She doesn't think I work."

"You don't."

My head falls to my chest. "I've had such a crap week."

"Your life is what you make it."

Rising from my chair at her table, I walk over to where she's standing by the stove. "Think of it as a night of not having to eat with Rhode. My mother never cooks. It'll probably be take-out. Plus birthday cake, I'm sure."

Her mouth swishes. "What kind of cake?"

I see an in. I need to answer this correctly. "Chocolate of course."

"Ice cream too?" she asks.

"Absolutely."

"What do I have to wear?"

"Will you please stop fidgeting? You're driving me crazy."

"You ain't wearing a dress. Why did I have to wear one?" Annie squirms in her seat.

I roll my eyes as I stop at a light. "I never told you to wear a dress. But to be honest, after I spent half the day watching you go through your closet, I'm just glad to see you in clothes."

"I didn't tell you to look at me naked."

"You left the door open and called me."

"I called you to tell you I was changing."

"You said my name and rattled something that I couldn't hear. How was I supposed to hear you? You mumble all the time."

"Mumble schmumble."

"See?" I say, pointing at her.

"If I knew you were gonna wear pants, I would have worn them too."

"There's no dress code. Plus, you didn't even try on pants today during the ridiculous fashion show you made me sit through."

"It's a party and I ain't nothing if not fashionable." She smooths out her dress and picks a piece of lint off her arm.

"Well, you look nice," I tell her.

She eyes me up and down. "Wish I could say the same for you."

I glare at her. "That's rude."

"Did you just throw something on? You need to take more time with your appearance. I've seen you in sweats, shorts, jeans, and yoga pants. No wonder that boy likes your sister. She must not be frumpy."

"Why do you start this shit with me? This is not what I need to hear."

"Calm your tits. Don't have a rack attack."

Shaking my head I glare at her. Where does she come up with this shit?

"You should change."

"If I change will you shut up?"

She shrugs. I glance down at my clothes. My mother will comment for sure. Maybe she's right. I make a U-turn and head to my apartment.

As soon as I park she speaks.

"I'll wait in the car."

"No, you will not. I'm not going up and down the stairs fifteen times so you can tell me that you don't like my outfit every time. Come on, let's get this over with," I say with a wave of my hand.

She huffs her way up the stairs. As soon as we reach my door, I spin on my heel to face her. "And by the way, if you think for one second I've forgotten the review you owe me, you're mistaken. I'm not dropping you off tonight until I get one."

She turns around and steps down. "I can take a cab then."

I reach for her arm and pull her back up the stair. I turn my key in the lock and gaze back at her. "Why can't you just say, 'Okay, Joss. Don't worry, I haven't forgotten.'"

"You gettin' bossy. I created a monster."

I flip on the switch and walk inside, dropping my purse on the couch. Annie is still in the doorway.

"Are you a vampire? Do I have to tell you you're welcome inside before you can cross the threshold?" I ask with a laugh.

"Lord have mercy. Did you get robbed?" she asks, placing her hand over her heart.

I roll my eyes. "I know it's a mess. I get busy."

"You busy being a slob. Child, no wonder you're single. There's probably a man buried in here somewhere and you don't even know it."

"What do you want me to wear? Can we please get this over with?" At this point, I'm not sure what's going to be worse, her dressing me or dinner with my family.

Annie slowly takes a few cautious steps inside the apartment. "Please tell me your clothes aren't on the floor."

"Not all of them."

Annie waves her hands in the air and spins out the door. I chase after her and pull her back by the arm.

"This was your idea."

"I didn't know your car was the Taj Mahal compared to your apartment. I'm gonna stand right here."

I roll my eyes and go in search of an Annie pleasing outfit. "So I assume if I wear something low cut you're going to hate it," I yell from the bedroom.

"You plannin' on hitting on one of your family members?"

"No."

"Then why you gotta show titties?"

"How about this one?" I ask, holding up a black dress.

"Did somebody die?"

"Black isn't just for funerals anymore."

"It's also not for birthday parties."

"Ugh."

Annie starts humming the "Cops" theme song and it makes me giggle.

"How about this one?" I ask. "It's blue."

"The color is okay."

"So it looks nice then?"

"How am I supposed to tell on a hanger? Put it on."

Returning to the bathroom, I'm happy to find it still fits me after all the food I've eaten this week. I step around the corner and Annie nods. "Yep. Now let's go."

"Yep? Not a 'Wow, you look nice?'"

Annie's already halfway to the car.

"I'll take that as a no." Why has my life suddenly become so complicated? Maybe bringing Annie was a bad idea. I hope I can get through this dinner without killing someone.

# CHAPTER Sixteen

"MOM, THIS IS ANNIE McClintonuck."

"When your father said you were bringing a friend, I assumed it was a man."

"I've got bigger balls than most men I know," Annie says as she clicks her teeth. She gazes around my mother's head toward the rear of the house. "You got a nice house. Looks clean. I can see Joslyn didn't take after you."

I roll my eyes. Annie's already selling me out and it's been less than a minute.

My mother smiles. "Oh, she's definitely nothing like me. Jane Walters." She holds out her hand to Annie and Annie shakes it.

"I didn't mean that like it was a good thing."

My mother's smile drops.

There's a moment of awkward silence and my mother breaks it. "Well, at least you dressed presentably for once."

"I'll take that as a compliment," I say. "Annie made me change or else I would have shown up in jeans."

"She has no style," my mother says to Annie.

"Oh, she got style, it's in her personality," Annie responds. Hmm, maybe I was wrong. She does have my back.

Laughter sounds from the back room and I recognize Jorgie's voice. I haven't spoken to her in a few days and I really want to talk to her about Rhode. I need to know all the things.

My dad comes around the corner and smiles brightly when he sees me. He pulls me into a hug. "Happy early birthday, sweet girl."

I relax into his hug. I didn't realize how much I needed one until just then. My dad always makes me feel better.

"You look beautiful!"

"Thank you."

"Dad, this is Annie. Annie, this is my father, John Walters."

"John and Jane?" Annie asks. "Good thing your last name wasn't Doe."

My dad smiles. "That's very true, Annie. Nice to meet you."

My mother rolls her eyes.

"Is that my snuggle bug princess I hear?"

I lean toward Annie and whisper, "Prepare yourself to meet your match."

Annie's eyes widen as my grandfather hops around the corner like the spring chicken he thinks he is.

He rushes over to me as much as he can with his limp and grabs me tightly, spinning me around. "Joss, joss bo boss, banana fanna foe floss, fee fi mo moss-Joss!"

"Hi, Grandpa."

His eyes meet Annie's. "Well, hello there. What do we have here? Did you bring me a snack?"

I press my lips together to avoid laughing as Annie takes a step back and clutches her purse to her chest.

"Wilbur Walters, this is Annie McClintonuck."

He holds out his hand to Annie. She sizes him up and down before cautiously reaching out to shake it. He quickly bends and presses his lips to her knuckles.

She pulls her hand back. "Get your dirty old lips off my skin. I ain't given you permission to taste me. I ain't no man's snack."

Wilbur grins from ear to ear. "You're absolutely right, darlin'. You're a five-course meal."

"Dad!" my mother shouts. "Really. Give the woman some space."

"She can have all the space in and around me," he replies, ogling Annie up and down.

"Come on in!" my father says awkwardly.

"Who are these people?" Annie grumbles.

"Jorgie, your sister is here. It's rude not to greet guests at the door."

"Sorry! I'm coming! Hey, sissy! Happy almost birthday!" She hugs me and whispers in my ear, "Thank God you're here. Mom is a nutjob on steroids tonight. Oh, and we need to talk."

I gaze into her eyes, trying to read her thoughts. I know she probably wants to tell me about Rhode and I'm dying to know how and why they hooked up.

As I open my mouth to agree with her, my mother says, "Oh, and you know Rhode Bennett."

"What?" I say, darting my head around Jorgie's to look behind her.

Sure as shit, Rhode is standing behind her holding a glass of soda.

"He, he, he. Shit just got real." Annie laughs.

"I hope you don't mind, but I invited Rhode tonight," Jorgie says with a smile.

I grit my teeth and attempt not to scowl. "Why would I mind?"

Rhode takes a deep breath and stares at me for a moment before his eyes move to Annie. "Annie! I didn't know I'd see you here. Did you get my message?"

"What message?" she asks.

I turn to face her and give her my biggest, nastiest face as I whisper, "I swear if you knew he was coming and didn't tell me . . ."

Annie clenches her jaw. "I ain't know nothin'," she mumbles back.

"I left a note on your door about an hour ago that I wasn't going to be able to make dinner. I got your machine at home."

She sneers at me. "I wasn't home. I was busy making sure Joss didn't lose a man in her apartment."

"What?" he asks.

I can't tell if he didn't hear her or he's jealous.

"Are we all going to stand in the doorway or can we please move into the dining room?" my mother announces, clearly aggravated.

Jorgie links her arm with mine as everyone begins to walk through the house. "I hope you don't mind I invited Rhode. I had to beg him to come tonight. He said he didn't think you'd want to see him. Why is that?"

"Are you happy?" I ask, turning to face her.

"Umm, yeah, I guess. Why?"

"Because as long as you're happy, nothing else matters, okay? You will always be my number one."

"I know that! You know I want you to be happy too, right?"

"I know you do. You just do whatever you have to do, okay? Don't worry about me. I'm fine."

"I ain't walkin' in there by myself," Annie says from behind me. "That man looks like he's going to eat me."

Following her line of sight, I see my grandfather curling his finger toward Annie, asking her to come. I chuckle. "He's harmless."

"Harmless like when there's a pin in your shirt. You don't even know it's there and then bam! You get stuck. He looks like he wants to stick me."

"I don't think we've met. I'm Joss's sister, Jorgie."

"Yeah, I heard all about you and your stealin' ways."

Jorgie's face drops into a worried frown. "Me?"

Nudging Annie with my elbow, I say, "She's a kidder. You'll get used to it."

"Oh, okay . . . Well, I'm glad I finally got to meet you. Thank you so much for the review you left on my website!"

Oh, shit.

"I left a review for you? What you talkin' 'bout?"

"Mom's going to get pissed if we don't get inside," I say, trying to break the conversation. I step behind Annie and shake my head to Jorgie, forming "No!" with my lips. She doesn't notice.

"My bakery. I opened on Monday. Joss said it's

down the street from your house."

Annie shoots questioning daggers in my direction. "Oh, yeah?" she asks. "Did your sister know I left you a review?"

I close my eyes and sigh. Jorgie finally realizes she's about to blow my cover. "Um, I don't . . . I mean . . . I don't think."

"Uh-huh. All right then, where's this cake? It better be worth my coming to this circus."

She marches past us and into the kitchen, where everyone has gathered.

"Crap! Should I not have said anything?" Jorgie asks, grabbing my arm.

"It's fine. Just enjoy yourself tonight."

"Me? This is your night!"

I smile politely. Oh. yeah. It's everything I dreamed and more.

# CHAPTER Seventeen

MY MOTHER'S SEATING ARRANGEMENT leaves a lot to be desired. At least I'm sitting next to my father. He and my mother are at the heads of the table. Annie is next to me and Wilbur insisted on sitting next to her. Rhode is directly across from me and Jorgie is next to him, closest to my mother.

"So, Joss, how did you and Annie meet?" my mother asks as she slices into the beef she ordered from across town. She acts like cooking is beneath her, but the truth is, she sucks at it.

"Annie has a large Internet presence and my magazine is interested in doing an article on how people go about leaving reviews for products and services."

"I really enjoyed the review you left on Hazel James' new romance novel *Saved* yesterday. It made me laugh," Jorgie says.

"I'm sorry, what?" I question, dropping my silverware on the table and turning to face Annie.

"This some good beef. Where's it from?" Annie asks my mother.

"I have some good beef too," Wilbur says, raising his eyebrows at Annie.

My mother is speechless. That's a first.

Annie holds up her knife. "You wanna pull it out? I'll slice it up right here and now, you dirty old fart!"

Wilbur chuckles. "You're my kind of woman, Annie. Are you seeing anyone?"

"What review?" I ask, tapping Annie on the shoulder. "Have you been leaving reviews and not telling me?" I guess I should have been checking up on her. Dammit.

"I dunno." She shrugs. "These beans are nice and crisp too," she says, focusing on her plate.

"I follow you on Amazon," Jorgie continues. "The review you left earlier today on salad tongs had me in stitches."

Annie shovels more beef into her mouth as I stare at her. I feel like I'm Mt. Vesuvius and about to blow.

"So, Rhode, how did you and Jorgie meet?" my father asks.

"You know this, John. Honestly, do you not listen to a word I say?" my mother says, shaking her head. "I told you they met when Joss brought him to the bakery."

"I'm Annie's neighbor."

My dad nods and continues to cut his veggies.

"Yeah, Joss found him and Jorgie stole him," Annie replies.

"Stole him? What?" Jorgie asks, eyes wide.

"No one stole anyone, Annie," I say, shaking my head at my sister and swirling my finger in a circle next to my head to show Annie's nuts.

Gazing up briefly at Rhode, I see his eyes boring into me. Why is he looking at me that way? My sister is right there.

His leg touches mine under the table and I gulp. He rubs my leg with his and smirks at me from across the table. My dad's leg mixes into ours. "Oops, sorry. Whose leg did I just hit?" he questions.

"That was mine, Mr. Walters. Sorry about that."

"You're tall. It happens. So how long have you been dating my daughter?" he asks.

I close my eyes and take a deep, painful breath.

"Which one?" Annie asks with a chuckle.

"I'm sorry, what?" my mother asks.

"Are you free tomorrow?" Wilbur asks Annie. "How about we go see a movie? Maybe make out a little?"

"Dad!" my mother shouts.

"I don't like you, you pervert. I ain't going nowhere with your ugly, old ass."

"Annie!" I say, shaking my head. I jump up from the table. "Excuse me, I need some ibuprofen. I have a headache."

"Let me help you," Rhode says, following me into the kitchen.

I open my purse and shift everything around with my fingers. Even my purse is a disorganized mess.

"Are you ever going to talk to me?" he asks.

I continue to shuffle around in my purse. "I know I put a bottle in here."

He places his hand over mine. I pause and gaze up at him. "Why are you in here talking to me right now? My sister is in there. You're her guest, not mine."

"I know she invited me, but I was hoping we could clear the air."

"The air is crystal clear, Rhode. Okay? Just forget about the whole thing. I'm sure I'm going to be seeing a lot more of you now and we should get along."

He leans his back on the counter as I start unloading the items from my purse.

"You think you'll be seeing more of me? Why is that?" he asks.

I find the bottle and try to pop the top, ignoring him. It seems glued on. I struggle with it and Rhode takes it from my hands, opens it with ease, and hands it back to me.

"So that guy, Adam. How long have you two been seeing each other?"

I stop and turn to face him. "Why do you care?"

"Really? Do you not want me to care about you?"

Counting out three pills, I toss them into my mouth and swallow. Then I begin restuffing my purse. "I want you to be good to my sister. You shouldn't think about me at all."

He smirks at me and licks his lips before gazing at the floor.

"You're an asshole, you know that?"

"Am I? Why is that?"

"Because you're seeing my sister and are in here with me. Pick a Walters girl and stick with her!"

"Joss, I'm not interested in your sister. I've never been."

My eyes widen. "If you hurt her, I'll chop off your dick and bury it in your garden!"

"Joss, everything okay in there?" my mother yells.

"Coming!"

Rhode steps in front of me blocking my path. My teeth clench.

"You really are gorgeous, especially when you're wrong."

My face tightens. "You're really a fucker, especially when you act like yourself."

I push past him and make my way back to the table.

Jorgie makes eye contact with me and then glances at Rhode as he enters the room. I hope she doesn't think something is going on with us. I feel like I need to tell her everything. I may keep secrets from everyone else, but never Jorgie. If Rhode doesn't have good intentions with her then she needs to know.

Rhode runs his fingers through his hair as he enters. He seems frustrated. Good. I'm going to blow his game sky high. He won't have either one of us.

"So, Annie, how long have you and Rhode been neighbors?" Jorgie asks.

"He moved in around five years ago. Hasn't left me alone since."

"I wouldn't leave you alone if I lived next to you either," Wilbur says with a wink. He's always been straightforward and a call-it-like-he-sees-it kind of guy, but I've never seen him so flirtatious.

"What's your deal?" Annie asks.

"Dad's a widower," my mom announces. "He's just messing with you, Annie. Ignore him."

"No, don't ignore me. But I'd like to mess with you if you'll let me."

Annie turns to me and her eyes beg for rescue. I can't help but start to laugh. Pretty soon everyone at the table is laughing but Annie. She says something under her breath and continues to eat her dinner quietly. It must be hard to swallow your own medicine.

After we bring the dishes into the kitchen, Jorgie pulls me by the arm. "Can we talk for a second?"

"Yes," I say, relieved. We walk down the hall, to my parents' bedroom.

"Sure! Leave me to do the dishes!" my mother shouts.

"She acts like putting plates in the dishwasher means doing the dishes," Jorgie says.

"I'm glad you wanted to talk to me. I need to warn you about Rhode," I begin.

"Oh?" she asks, concerned.

"He's not what he appears to be. I think he's a player."

"Really? I didn't get that impression at all."

I flop down on the bed and she sits next to me.

"I hope you didn't mind that I asked him to come tonight."

I shake my head and glance up at the ceiling. How do I say this to her without hurting her?

"He seems like a really good guy, Joss. He came to see me at the bakery the other day, you know?"

"Yeah. I saw you two."

"You did? I didn't see you."

"I didn't want to interrupt. It seemed like you two were having a moment."

She smiles. "We were. No one has ever made that

much effort. I think you know what that means." She seems almost giddy as she squirms and shakes her legs.

My chest hurts again and I can't look at her.

"What? What's wrong?" she asks, touching my arm. "Do you not like him?"

"I do. I mean, yeah, I did. But Jorgie . . . he told me tonight he's not interested in you."

Her head flinches back and she scratches her cheek. "I never thought he was."

"I don't want him to hurt you! I'm so sorry."

She clutches at my arm and snorts. "Wait. Do you think I like him?"

"Don't you?"

"Well, yeah, but only because I've never had a guy come to me for advice about my sister before. I think it's endearing."

My mouth drops. "He did what?"

"Oh my gosh, Joss. Did you think I brought him here because I'm interested in him?" Her voice cracks as she presses her hand against her heart. "He came to the bakery that morning because he wanted advice on how to ask you out."

My lips quiver with excitement. "Are you serious?"

"Yes!" she says as she rolls her eyes. "Joss, he's so into you!"

I stand and begin to pace. "But, I was at his house and things got really flirtatious. I tried to kiss him and he pulled away from me like I had two heads."

"I think he's old-fashioned," she says with a smile. "I got the feeling from what he said that he didn't want you to think he was only interested in your body."

"Holy fuck!" Reviewing all our conversations, I

start to feel like the idiot that I am.

"I had to beg him to come tonight. He said you were mad at him and didn't want to see him. I told him you were complicated and not to give up on you. He said, and I quote, 'I knew there was something special about her from the moment I met her.'"

"Gah!" I screech. "What do I do?"

She belly laughs and rolls back on the bed, raising her hands in the air. "Go get him!"

I rush from the bedroom door, not knowing what I'm going to say to him. I owe him an apology at bare minimum. But mostly, I want to kiss him. I've never had someone make me so angry yet draw me in at the same time. My mother is still huffing as she places the plates in the dishwasher.

"Where's Rhode?" I ask.

"Honestly, Joss. I'm slaving away in here. Is it my responsibility to know where everyone is and what they're doing? You haven't even thanked me for putting this together."

"Thanks," I say as I rush past her.

Once I'm in the living room, I scan the room for him. Annie is sitting on a chair and Grandpa is smiling at her and waving to her from the couch, patting the seat next to him like she should come sit by him. Dad is flipping channels on the TV. Rhode is nowhere to be found.

Annie jumps up when she sees me. "Don't you leave me alone with this dirty fart again!"

"Where's Rhode?" I ask.

"He got a call. Said there was some problem with work he had to take care of and left."

My heart drops.

"What?" she questions, folding her arms.

"I'm an idiot of epic proportions!"

She nods and twists her mouth. "I could have told you that!"

Choosing to ignore her comment, I walk over to the couch and sit down next to my grandfather. "He went to see Jorgie to ask about me. She brought him here to help get us together."

Annie tilts her head to the side and clicks her teeth. "I like her more now."

I lean my head on my grandfather's shoulder and he puts his arms around me.

He pats me on the back. "What's got you down, cupcake?"

"Did you ever do something dumb and not know how to make it right?"

"Being young is about making mistakes and learning from them. As long as your heart is in the right place, there's nothing that can't be fixed. I just told that young man the same thing."

I kiss him on the cheek and notice Annie watching us. I point to him on the sly and raise my eyebrows at her. She waves me off and leaves the room.

What a night. I have some fixing to do.

# CHAPTER Eighteen

I PULL MY HOOD up over my head as I make my way to Annie's front porch. It's been pouring for the last two hours and everything is a wet, muddy mess. Even though it's morning, it almost feels like evening since it's so dark and dreary outside.

Glancing over at Rhode's house, I wonder if he's home. I don't know what I'm going to say to him when I see him, but I suppose I'll start with I'm sorry followed by I have the hots for you.

I tap on Annie's door and walk in as usual. I have a few things I want to say to Annie too. I was too tired to bring up the reviews after I left my parents' last night, but to say I'm pissed off that she's been writing and posting reviews without telling me would be an understatement. She's going to hear just how much.

I walk through the door and Annie's rear end is up in the air. She's on the floor, looking under the couch.

"Did you lose something?" I question. "Maybe all those reviews you told me you never wrote?"

She ignores me as she rushes into her bedroom. I follow her. She's on her hands and knees again, looking under the bed.

"What's going on?" I ask.

"I can't find him!"

"Who?"

"Stupid. He's gone. I can't find him anywhere."

I drop my bag on the floor and join her looking under the bed. "When was the last time you saw him?"

"I don't know. Last night, I think. He was on the chair when I got home."

"He's got to be around here somewhere."

She walks into the kitchen and opens a can of cat food. "Stupid? Come here, you lousy cat!"

I see the panic on her face, so I begin to open doors and look in closets.

She starts to pace and rub her hands on her legs.

"It's going to be all right. We'll find him."

"What if he got out?" she asks.

"Do you think he could have?"

"I don't know." She stops to think, pressing the back side of her hand to her forehead. "I opened the front door to get the paper. Now that I think of it, I stumbled as I came back in. I thought nothing of it because I stumble a lot these days. Oh, Lord Jesus. What if he ran out? He can't see. It's raining!"

I tug on my bottom lip with my fingers. "I'll go out and look for him."

"Oh, damn that cat! He's going to kill me!" She places her hand on her chest.

"Sit down. Relax. How long ago did you get the paper?"

"About a half-hour ago."

"Okay, he can't be far. I'll go out and look for him.

Do you have some treats or something he might like?"

She points to the pantry door and wrings her hands. I've never seen her so upset. I say a silent prayer he's okay as I grab a bag of treats with catnip. "I'll be back soon."

"Find my baby!"

I nod my head as I walk out her door. It's pouring and I have no idea where to look. I start in her back-yard.

The rain makes it hard to see. I look behind bushes and under the bench. "Here, kitty kitty!"

"Did you find him?"

I turn to see Rhode in a drenched T-shirt and jeans standing behind me.

"Did she tell you?" I ask.

"Yeah, she called me a few minutes ago. I looked all over this side of the street. I saw your car, so I thought I'd circle back."

"She's so upset. I've never seen her this way."

"I know."

"We have to find him, Rhode!"

"We will. Come on, there's a park down the street. Let's look there."

We search under cars on the street and look up trees as we make our way to the park. I go to the opposite side of the road and he stays on the right. We both call his name as we walk.

Rhode gets on his knees to look under a truck. "Anything?" I shout from the other side, raising my hands in the air.

"No! Let's keep going."

After a few minutes we get to the park. It's just off

a main road and traffic flies past us on the street. The idea of him getting hit by a car makes my stomach curl. We need to find him fast.

"He's probably hiding somewhere. Cats don't like water," he says as he pushes his wet hair out of his face.

I nod. "Okay. Where would he hide?" I shout over a boom of thunder.

"You take over there and I'll check here," he says, pointing to a path through the trees.

I glance behind bushes and rattle the bag of treats, calling his name. "Stupid! Where are you, Stupid?" I make puckering noises with my mouth. "Here, kitty, kitty!"

The rain is coming down in buckets. My shoes are drenched and I can tell my shirt is getting soaked through the lightweight coat I threw on this morning. But none of that is more important than finding Annie's cat. She might say she hates him, but just like everything else, I get the feeling she hates the things she actually loves. Maybe Rhode was right about her from the start.

"Joss!" He shouts my name and I take off running down the path.

"Where are you? I don't see you."

"Down here!"

I follow the sound of his voice down a steep hill and see him on his knees by a drain tube. "He's here!" he says with a smile. "But he won't come out!"

I slide down the hill, tracking mud up my legs as I move. He reaches out his hand for me and I take it. I crouch down to look in the tunnel. Stupid meows.

"Oh, thank God! We were so worried about you!"

Rhode puts his hand on my back. "See if he'll come out for a treat."

I rattle the bag and open it, taking out a piece. In my most baby voice I say, "Ooh . . . look what I have. Mmm . . . want some?"

Rhode chuckles and I realize how dumb I must sound. "What? Do you think he'd respond better to shouting?"

He laughs. "Well, he does live with Annie!" He shrugs as he places his dirty hands on his knees.

"You're right!"

I turn back to face Stupid. "Get your dumb ass outta there or you'll never eat again!" I shout, using my best Annie voice.

"That was pretty good. I'm impressed."

I giggle. "I've spent a lot of time with her."

Our eyes lock on each other and I can feel the heat between us. His smile fades as he stares at my mouth. The water drips down his face and I desperately want to reach out and wipe it away, just to touch him. He breaks our eye contact to refocus on the problem at hand. Gazing down at the ground, I remember I have so much I want to say to him, but I know it's not the time. I hope he gives me a chance to apologize.

He bends down next to me. "I think I'm going to have to crawl in there and get him."

"Will you fit?" I ask. It's kind of narrow."

"It's worth a shot."

I back up and he lies flat on the ground. He wriggles and twists his way in but can't get past his chest.

"Shit! I'm too big!"

"Let me try!" I say as he pushes himself out.

I take out a treat and hand the bag to him. I lie on the ground and start to slide into the dark hole. "Come here, baby. It's okay. It's me, Joss."

He meows lightly and I can tell he's scared.

I slide deeper into the tunnel and as I get closer, he backs up.

"No!"

"What?" Rhode asks, lying down beside me, trying to see over my head.

"He's scared."

"Sometimes fear makes you run from the thing you need the most."

Turning my head toward him, I wonder if he's talking about me now. I refocus on the cat. "Come here, Stupid. It's okay."

Holding the treat in my palm, I slowly move it closer to him. I can make out his whiskers from the light from a crack in the tube. He seems to be sniffing the air.

"That's it. Look what I have for you. Come on! I think he's coming. That's it, baby. Come on."

"Do you have him?" Rhode asks.

"I'm going to grab him when he gets closer. When I say the word, you're going to have to pull me out. Can you do that?"

"Just tell me when."

I feel his hands on my thighs and I try not to think about how it feels even though chills race through my body.

Stupid inches toward me. I know I only have one shot at this. He takes the catnip and I grab him by the neck. He meows and struggles. "Now, Rhode! Now!"

He pulls my legs and I slide out with the cat. He quickly grabs him and holds him as I push up. I'm completely covered in mud.

"Great job, babe. You did it."

He called me babe. My heart pounds in my chest. I'm glad we found the cat, but right now I'm certain my heart is beating for the man in front of me.

There's another boom of thunder and Stupid struggles in Rhode's arms.

"Here, give him to me!" I say, motioning with my hands. I unzip my jacket and place him inside of it, holding tightly.

"Let's get the hell out of here."

I glance up the hill. "I don't know if I can," I tell him, slightly worried. "I have to hold on to Stupid and it's steep."

He pushes his damp hair from his eyes with his muddy hands and I can tell he's thinking. "You go first. You can lean into me. I'll stand behind you in case you lose your balance."

I start to climb and I feel his hands on my waist helping me up. We run back to Annie's in the rain, laughing the whole time.

He rings her doorbell and the dog chimes bark.

Annie quickly opens the door and I hold out Stupid in front of me. He almost looks brown now that he's got so much dirt on him.

"Where in the hell have you been?" she asks as she takes him from my hands.

She walks inside, closes the door, and I hear it lock.

Rhode and I stare at each other in disbelief.

I cup my hand next to my mouth and yell, "You're welcome!"

He bends down at his knees to catch his breath and laughs. I shake my head and look down at my hands. There's mud under my nails, up my arms. It's everywhere.

"Shit!" I say, glancing back at my car. "Do you have a towel I can borrow to sit on when I drive home?"

He shakes his head. "You can't go home like that. Come with me." He takes my hand and pulls me before I have a chance to answer him. I don't want to leave him anyway. I have a lot I need to say.

We run through the rain back to his house. He feels around his pockets for his keys. I see the panic in his expression.

"Oh, no!" I shout, laughing.

"Fuck! Hold on."

He finally pulls them from his pants pocket and sighs in relief. We go through his front door and shake the water off. It's nice to be out of the rain. I'm not sure why, but I start to shiver.

He notices. "You're cold. Wait here." He kicks off his shoes and tiptoes through the house. A few seconds later he returns with a pile of towels.

"Let's take that off," he says, unzipping my jacket.

He pulls it off my arms and wraps a towel over my shoulders. I take off my wet shoes and place them by the door on the mat. He lifts his T-shirt from the bottom and pulls it over his head, revealing a dirty, wet, chiseled six pack that makes my mouth water.

I'm still shaking, but now I think it's more from being with him.

"W-o-w," I say as I stare at him, voice shaking as my teeth chatter.

He stares at me and glances down at himself. "I'm filthy."

"That's not what I was wowing over."

His lips curl as he rubs his hands over my arms. "Let's get you in the shower."

Taking me by the hand, he leads me through the house into his bedroom where he carefully pulls a robe from his closet using the tips of his fingers. I follow him into the bathroom and he turns on the water. I'm still shaking.

"You need to get out of those wet clothes."

"What about you?" I ask.

"I'm okay."

"You're more than okay," I say, meeting his gaze. His head tilts to the side to regard me. My teeth vibrate as I try to say what I need to say. "I'm sorry," I tell him. "Jorgie explained everything last night. I came out of the bedroom to apologize to you and you were already gone."

"It was a misunderstanding. No big deal."

"It's a big deal to me. I thought you two were dating."

"Yeah, I figured that out. I just don't know why you'd think that."

"Because she's her and you're, well . . ." I motion up and down at his body. "And you're *that.*"

He gazes down at himself. "I'm what? A dirty mess?"

"Yeah. A hot dirty mess."

"You think I'm hot?" he says with a wink.

I suddenly feel shy. I know I'm blushing, so I gaze at the floor.

His fingers lift my chin. "Joss, I really am a mess. You just don't see it. And I like you, a lot. The other day things got kind of crazy . . . and damn, I knew I was flirting. I really, really wanted to be with you. But see, I've done that before. I've had relationships based on sex and I didn't want that with you. I didn't want you to think that's all it was for me. You're different."

"You could have told me that while we had sex."

He runs his fingers through his hair and looks me over. I assume it's because everything is stuck to my skin the way it's stuck to his, leaving very little to the imagination.

"If you only knew. I've wanted you since I saw you in that bar."

"Then take me," I tell him, stepping toward him.

He closes his eyes and sighs. "Can I take you on a date first?"

"Are you serious?" My teeth stop chattering.

"That day you were at work with Annie, I called you to ask you out. I never had a chance because, well, something happened and things got all weird. Then you were here in my house in those short shorts and so beautiful. I couldn't think straight."

"I make it hard for you to think?"

"Yes," he says, taking a deep breath. "Every time I come close to you, I lose all sense of reason."

I drop the towel from my shoulders and remove my T-shirt. "How about now?"

"Joss . . ." His words say stop but his eyes want more.

I start to unzip my jeans.

"If you take off those jeans, I'm going to ruin everything."

I smirk as I tug them down my legs, gazing up at his face. "Why, are you a lousy lay?"

He shakes his head and I watch his lips curl slightly on the side. "I'm going to be the best you've ever had. *After* I take you on a date."

I drop my pants to the floor and he gazes up at the ceiling.

"Your shower has been running for a while. Pretty soon, you're going to be out of hot water. Since we both need to get cleaned up I think we should conserve and take one together."

"You're making this really hard."

I bite my lip. "I hope I'm making something hard."

I undo the clasp of my bra and slowly pull it down my shoulders, not revealing my breasts. He can't help but watch me, even though he tries to act like he's not.

"How about we take a shower and after we can have lunch. We'll call it a date. Unless there's somewhere else you'd rather be." Covering my nipples with my fingers, I let my bra fall to the floor. I step past him and into the shower. Once I'm hidden behind the curtain, I remove my underwear and glance out the curtain to see he's facing the door. I toss them at him and they hit him in the back. I can see him inhale sharply. "Totally up to you."

I pull the shower curtain closed and step under the water, silently praying. I didn't know I had that in me. I hear the bathroom door close and lower my head. Wrong again. What was I thinking? Just as I'm about to allow myself to feel like a loser, the shower curtain pulls back and a naked Rhode steps inside with me.

"Hi," he says in a whisper.

"I didn't think you were coming." I can't help but smile shyly.

He lifts his hand and wipes dirt from my cheek.

"I'm not letting you get the wrong idea again. I've always wanted you, but so you know, you're going to have to see a lot more of me from here on out." His eyes lower as he scans my body. When did I ever think he was shy?

As my fingers trail down his chest to his stomach then his package, I bite my lip. "I definitely like seeing more of you."

He reaches for the bar of soap and runs his hands over it repeatedly, creating a lather as he stares me up and down. "There's so much dirt. I have my work cut out for me."

"I expect you to clean every inch of me. I'm pretty sure there's dirt even in places you can't see."

I'm usually not this confident. I don't know what's gotten into me. There's something about how he looks at me that makes me feel like I'm the most beautiful girl in the world. Knowing he thinks I'm hot gives me extra confidence. Leaning my head backward, I let the water rush over my hair. The water trickles down my neck and my breasts. I run my hands over myself and stare into his eyes.

His eyes darken and I know that if I ask, I can probably have anything I want at this moment. He steps into the water with me. His soapy hands caress my shoulders as he carefully washes them. My skin tingles under his touch.

He gazes down at my breasts as his hands trail from my neck to my chest. He washes each breast carefully, paying soft attention to my nipples. I'm starting to shake again, but this time the vibration is coming from my core.

I reach out and take the soap in my hands. His shoulders are broad and muscular. I have to touch him.

His hands trail down my stomach to my belly button and he moans as he reaches my hips.

I knead my soapy fingers into his shoulder blades and he relaxes under my touch. His eyes meet mine and I can't help but stare at his mouth.

He steps closer to me until my breasts are against his bare chest. Gazing down into my eyes, he runs the back of his fingers against my cheek. Seconds feel like minutes as I wait and beg for his mouth with my eyes.

His lips gently touch mine and it's more than I imagined.

Curling his hand up my back to my neck, he pulls my face toward his.

His kiss is soft and tender. But his hard dick flicks against my leg. I smile as he kisses me and he returns the expression knowingly.

"You wanted me hard."

"I want everything hard."

He gives me exactly what I need as his tongue invades my mouth. He's no longer tender. His tongue licks mine and I gently suck it to let him know all the things I want to do to him.

He groans. "I've never met anyone like you. Do you always say what you want?"

"If I tell you I want you inside me, will you go there?"

"I'm done saying no to you."

"Then give me everything."

His lips crash against mine as he devours my mouth with his. Grabbing ahold of his back, I knead my fingers into his flesh before trailing them down to his ass. It feels even better than I thought it would.

I lift my leg and he pushes me into the shower wall, pressing his hips into me. I feel his tip at my entrance and I bend slightly to give him access.

His dick slides into me and we both moan out loud as his tongue molds with mine. He feels so good inside me, I never want it to end.

He breaks the bond by lifting my legs around his waist. He turns off the water and yanks open the shower curtain. The cold air hits my warm skin and goosebumps break out all over my body.

He carries me out of the bathroom and slowly drops me onto his bed.

"I'm going to get your sheets dirty," I say as he stands over me and reaches into his nightstand for protection. I gaze down at my body and his. We're both still covered in mud.

"The dirtier the better," he says as he climbs over me and uses his hands to spread my legs.

"Ooh!" I say with surprise. He's strong and forceful. I like it.

"Here's what's going to happen," he begins as he presses the tip of his penis into my folds.

I arch my back and try to pull him in, but he won't

let me.

"I'm going to make love to you. Then we're going to clean up, have food, and I'm going to eat your pussy for dessert. Understand?"

I nod because it's all I can do. He might just be the most perfect man I've ever known. No one has ever left me at a loss for words.

"Is that a yes, Joss?"

"Fuck yes, it's a yes."

He slowly pushes into me and I'm reminded of how long it's been. My girly parts scream out in happiness as he claims my body the way he's already claimed my heart.

# CHAPTER Nineteen

"THAT WAS THE BEST dessert I've ever had," I say with a laugh as I roll over to face him, leaning my head on his chest.

"I'd have to agree with you there," he replies, kissing my forehead.

After we ate lunch, we washed our clothes, showered for real, and changed his sheets. Then he kept his word.

"Holy hell! It's almost one!" I shout when I notice the clock on the nightstand.

"Yeah, we've been at it for a while."

"I need to get over to Annie's. I need those reviews."

I try to sit up and he pins me down, crawling on top of me.

"Why is this so important to you?"

"This story? It's my chance at showing my boss, Darla, that I have what it takes to be a writer."

"And the magazine thinks a story on how people do reviews will draw interest?"

Turning my face away from his, I stare at the wall.

I haven't been truthful with him and now I'm worried about what will happen when he finds out what I'm really up to.

"What is it?" he asks, concerned.

"How did you and Annie meet? I mean, you're so protective of her. How did that happen?"

He pushes up and sits on the bed next to me. "I moved here a few years ago. I lived in Texas most of my life, but I'd decided I needed to branch out on my own. Annie was . . . well, she was Annie and it was refreshing. I instantly liked her."

"Was she nicer back then?"

"Nice is a relative term, don't you think? Annie says what she thinks and I respect that. But I also feel like she does it to protect her heart and I get that too."

Pulling his bedsheet around my chest, I sit up to see him better. "What do you mean?"

"My father is a professor. A Rhodes scholar," he says, making quotation marks with his fingers around the word Rhodes. "He wanted more from me than I could give him and after a while, I stopped caring about his feelings to protect my own."

"What did he want from you?"

"He wanted me to be a doctor like him. He didn't care what kind, so he said, but I think he wanted me to go into medicine. Torrance Bennett needed a son who measured up to the family name."

He lies across the bed and leans on his arm. "I was always fascinated by nature. I knew I loved planting things and watching them grow. My passion has always been seeing the potential in something small and seemingly insignificant and knowing someday with care it could be so much more."

I smile at him as he speaks. He has the same intensity in his eyes as I do when I talk about writing.

"But dear old dad wasn't happy with that. He'd never come right out and say it. He'd sashay around his feelings and use innuendo to get his point across. I told him I wanted to start a landscaping business. He told me I should go into horticulture and teach. He wanted me to get my doctorate. I got my bachelor's and I was done. He knew I liked working with my hands. There's no way in hell I could stand wearing suits and sitting at a desk all day. It's not who I am."

Touching his hands with my fingers, I admire every callus. We both use our hands, just in different ways.

"I would have rather he came right out and told me he hated the idea rather than grimacing every time I talked about it. I think it's one of the reasons I liked Annie immediately when I met her. She told me she didn't like me within the first minute we met. Of course, now I know she doesn't mean any of it. But I would have rather my father just come out and say he didn't like who I became, or that he was disappointed in me rather than have to read between the lines my entire life."

Pulling my knees to my chest, I stare down at him on the bed. "Your father and my mother make quite a pair."

He reaches up and pushes a strand of hair from my eyes.

"So Annie said she didn't like you? That doesn't surprise me. How did you end up cutting her grass?"

He sighs and sits up to face me. "Her yard was a disaster. There were weeds everywhere. Her bushes were out of control. I couldn't stand it. I got the feeling either she didn't care about how it looked or couldn't keep up with it. When I saw the inside of her house for the first time, I knew it was the latter. I told her how much I loved yardwork and begged her to let me take care of it. She waved me off and I took that as a yes."

He really is a good guy. I know it in my heart. It makes me feel even worse about what I'm doing. What if he gets mad at me?

"You okay?" he asks. "You do that a lot."

"What?"

"Get that far off distant look in your eyes. What's going on in that head of yours?"

"Wouldn't you like to know," I say with a smile.

"I would."

I can't help but watch his mouth move as he speaks. The stubble around his lips is the perfect length. It feels so good when he kisses me and frames the amazing lips I suddenly need to kiss again.

Reaching out with my hands, I pull his face to mine and press my lips to his. A soft kiss changes into a deeper kiss and before I know it, I'm lying on top of him.

I pull back and sigh. "I can't start this again."

"You kissed me," he says, lifting his hands in the air as if he's innocent.

"I know, and as much as I want to kiss you all day long, I really do need to go." I stand up and stretch my arms above my head. I turn to face him and he's grinning.

"Let me date you."

His words take me by surprise. "Isn't that what

we're doing?"

I walk out of the room to check if my clothes are done in the dryer.

He follows me, equally naked, through the house. "I'm serious."

"I know you are." I pull out my underwear and slide it up my legs. "So am I."

He watches me for a moment then tilts his head to the side. He's freaking adorable.

"So what do you say?" he asks.

"I say you can mow my lawn anytime you want." Clasping my bra, I reach for my jeans. They're nice and warm.

"Really? So this was about sex with you?"

I stop dressing and lean into him. "Of course not." He doesn't seem to believe me so I feel I need to explain.

"Do you know how many actual relationships I've had in my life? One. One that lasted longer than a few months and that was in high school. I don't know how to do this. Sex is all I've ever known. To me, this feels like dating because I already know so much about you."

He locks his fingers around my waist and holds me against him. I roll my fingers over his tanned chest. His eyes darken and I sense things are about to take a more serious turn. As much as I want to be with him, I start to feel scared.

"Joss, I'm not going to lie to you and tell you I know what I'm doing either because I don't. I've never actually wanted to date someone until I met you."

"Is that a good thing?" I ask nervously.

"A very good thing. I just need to know if you want more, too."

"I can tell you with absolute honesty that I know I think about you way too much."

"That's not an answer, Joss."

Pulling my shirt over my head, I kiss his lips once more. "You don't really know me. What if you don't like me when you do?" I try to sound confident but inside the question burns. The real question is whether or not he'll still like me when he finds out my true motives with Annie. I'm secretly afraid I'm already too close to him. If he finds out my truth and leaves me, I don't know if I'll recover. I need to protect my heart.

"I don't think that will happen."

"You don't know that. I don't want to get hurt."

I turn toward the door and he pulls me back. "Hey, do you remember what I said to you earlier in the bathroom? How I wanted to wait and date you? I still do. Don't let this make you think otherwise."

I bite my lip and gaze down at his perfect body. "You should never ever wear clothes."

I rush toward the front door and blow him a kiss.

He shakes his head and leans on the doorframe. "I'm going to date the shit out of you," he yells as I shut the door behind me.

I close my eyes for a moment and lean my back against his door. I don't want to admit it out loud, but deep down I know I want everything with him. It's like I was his from the minute I saw him. Something inside me is changing and I like the way it feels. But I know I'm not being honest and it's holding me back. I feel sick over the whole thing. Maybe I should walk away.

Could I do that?

Gazing up at the sky, I beg, "Please don't let me ruin this." As I make my way to Annie's, I know in my heart, I'm going to destroy it.

# CHAPTER Twenty

"ANNIE, OPEN UP! WE need to talk."

"Whatchoo yellin' for?" she asks as she rounds the corner of the house.

I step down off the porch. "Where were you just now?"

"I'm going to work. Harold needs me for a couple of hours." She holds out my bag. I almost forgot all about it. When I don't take it, she drops it to the ground.

"Wait, but we need to talk."

She waves her hands in the air and marches toward her car. I pick up my purse, rush over, and jump in the passenger seat.

"Oh no, you don't!"

"If you're going to work, then so am I. Do you realize this is supposed to be our last day together?"

"Not my fault you weren't around."

"You know damn well where I was! I was looking for Stupid. You're welcome, by the way."

She eyes me up and down. "You aren't dirty no more."

"Well, I was filthy no thanks to you. You didn't

even offer me a paper towel."

She smiles as she places the car in reverse. "I knew lawnmower man had something for you to wipe your face on."

I do a double take at her and force myself to look out her window to avoid smiling.

"Ahh!" she says, pointing her finger at me and poking my arm. "I knew it. Who owes who a thank you now?"

"Whatever happened, assuming anything happened, has nothing to do with you." I cross my arms.

"How was it?" she asks as she turns the corner and stops at a light.

I gaze out the window.

"I'm not blind. That boy has a body like a truck. If I were younger I would've gone after him myself."

I roll my eyes at her but can't help but laugh picturing them as a couple.

"He's a pain in the ass. I hope you're taking him off my hands."

My inner dialogue rages in my mind. I need to get at least some of my worries off my chest before I explode. "I don't know if it's going to work out."

"Why?"

I shrug.

"Child, you didn't go this far to give up on your dreams. Sometimes you have to do what you have to do. Not everyone is going to like your decisions, but it's your life."

Turning to face her, I feel like we aren't talking about the same thing. I look away and bite on my nail. I don't know how to respond to that and I feel as if I'll get myself into trouble if I do, so I zip my lips for the rest of the drive.

We pull into the dollar store parking lot and she turns off the ignition. I need to make sure she knows I haven't forgotten.

"Annie, we need to talk about these reviews."

"I gotta work now."

Pressing my fingernails into my palms as she huffs her way inside, I decide to take this time to think through exactly what I'm going to say to her and how best to say it. I'll wait until after her shift rather than lose my cool in front of her coworkers.

I follow her into the store and am proud when I walk past a large section of potato chips and don't feel the need to stuff my face.

"Ms. Joss!" Harold shouts as he wheels a cart over to me. "You come in to get some things?"

"Not today."

He seems disappointed.

"Do you mind if I hang out with Annie? I promise I won't keep her from working. I don't want you to fire her."

"Fire her?"

"Yeah. I know she really likes this job."

He moves closer to me and waves me away from the register. "If I tell you something you have to promise me you won't say a word to Annie."

I nod.

"'Cause ain't no one want Annie pissed off at them. Know what I mean?"

"More than you know."

He glances over both shoulders and whispers, "I

don't pay Annie to work. She volunteers."

"What?" I question, certain I heard him wrong.

"Annie and I go to the same church. She asked me if she could come here a couple of days a week and help stock the shelves. I told her I couldn't pay her and she said she didn't mind. She said she just wanted to get out of the house. I understand that. It's not easy being alone all the time."

"She said you called her in to work today."

"Nope. She called and asked if she could come in. I got the impression she was trying to avoid something. Do you know what that could be?"

"Yeah. I'm guessing it's me. How much do you know about her?"

"Well . . . she's pretty private. I know she was going to get married a few years ago and it didn't happen. I heard he ran off on her then got hit by a train or something."

A cold chill runs through my body. I hope that was an expression and not the truth. The look on his face tells me truth.

"His sister was her best friend. I guess they all worked together at some greeting card place. Annie takes care of her now. Visits her all the time. I can't think of her name." He taps his temple and looks up at the ceiling.

"Thea?"

"Yeah, Thea. That's her. Bobby's little sister. Do you know her?"

"I've met her a couple of times. Are you sure you have your facts straight?" I ask. "I thought Bobby had a heart attack."

He shakes his head. "Not that I know of. Only one with heart problems was Annie. He broke it. Everybody said she was never the same."

My lungs constrict in my chest. It feels hard to breathe. "Thanks for telling me, Harold."

"Now don't you tell Annie. She'd have me strung up on the roof hangin' by my man parts, if you know what I mean."

I smile. "I do. Don't worry. I won't say a word."

I pat him on the shoulder as I slowly walk down the aisle. I felt certain I knew all there was to know about Annie McClintonuck. Replaying everything in my mind, I try to force myself into not feeling sorry for her. She's lied about everything. I've paid her a shit-ton of money to tell me about her reviews and she told me she hadn't written any. Then yesterday, I find out she's been writing and posting them all along. Who does that shit? She's lied about a lot of things for no reason at all. I refuse to feel sorry for her. I have to remind myself that her main purpose is to cause pain. It seems like she wants everyone else to feel what she feels. That's not fair.

I fire myself up inside. We all have shit that happens in our lives. It doesn't give us any right to destroy other people just to make ourselves feel better.

I round a corner and see Annie placing Hostess Ding Dongs on the shelf.

"Who came up with this name?" she says to me as I approach. "You ever think about that? I wonder if when they were tryin' to think of what to call it, the creator threw one at his partner and said, 'You ain't nothin' but a ding dong.'"

I force a smile.

"What's got your goat?" she asks. "Trouble in cunnilingus court already?"

"Annie, when are you going to explain to me why you posted all those reviews and told me you hadn't written any?" My plan to wait to talk to her later flies out the window along with my patience.

She raises an eyebrow at me and gives me a glassy stare. "Your sister is crazy. I didn't leave no new reviews."

"Please don't lie to me."

"Oh, really? You wanna talk about lying? How about you tell me when you knew I'd left a review for her bakery?"

My muscles tense and I clear my throat. "Maybe we should discuss this when you're done working."

"Uh-huh. Maybe we should."

She returns to stocking the shelf and my phone vibrates in my pocket.

Walking toward the front entrance, I answer the call without looking at the ID. "Hello."

"I was thinking you and I should go on a date again soon."

I smile. "Didn't you have enough of me earlier?"

"Earlier? You mean the other night?"

I glance down at the number and see it's Adam, not Rhode. I didn't realize how similar their voices were until just now. "Yeah, um, the other night. That's what I meant." My capacity for sticking my foot in my mouth knows no bounds.

"So what do you say? Can I pick you up again tonight?"

"Adam, I need to tell you something. I'm kinda seeing—"

"I did some research for you on that Annie chick. I think you'd find it really interesting."

I pause. "What did you find?"

"How about I come over to your place tonight and I'll tell you what I know."

The last thing I want is to spend another second with Adam, but if he has information that could help me, isn't it my journalistic responsibility to pursue every avenue? My drive to succeed wins over my heart. "Fine. I'll see you at seven."

I hang up the phone before I can change my mind. I promise myself that as soon as he tells me what he knows, I'll be honest with him about my feelings. But what exactly am I feeling?

When I thought it was Rhode calling I was so happy. I can't remember ever feeling happy before I met him. Was I? He's a really good person. I want to be good. He makes me want to be better for him. I scratch my head and walk outside. I don't deserve him.

It's stopped raining, but it's still a gloomy day. I like a dark day sometimes. Right now, the sky matches my heart. Today is my last day with Annie and probably the last time she'll ever willingly talk to me. If I can figure out how to make this story work, this article gets published, and he figures out who I really am, Rhode will probably want nothing to do with me either. Darla is going to expect something from me come Monday morning. What am I going to do?

I functioned just fine before I met them. Why should I worry about how they feel? I'm doing my job.

Do I need them in my life? I pace outside the store. Why am I suddenly so unsure about everything?

How many people have ever looked out for what I need besides me? I've been on my own for what seems to be my whole life, fighting my way through it all. I've made myself into everything I am by working hard and making sacrifices. Why should I stop now when I'm so close?

Reaching into my purse, I lift out my notebook and read through the notes I've been keeping since this whole thing began. As I flip through the pages, I can see how naïve I was. "Angry Annie doesn't care about anyone but herself. She's a greedy old woman who carries a torch of hatred for everything around her. She's the epitome of an Internet troll." Is that how I feel now that I've gotten to know her?

I can't second-guess myself. I have a job to do and I need to finish what I started. Screw all these feelings. I'm probably just confused. Darla wants an exposé and that's exactly what she's going to get.

# CHAPTER Twenty-one

WE DON'T SPEAK ON the way back to Annie's house. I follow her inside and she doesn't say a word when I flop down on her couch.

Stupid swirls around my legs. He's clean now and purring. I pick him up and kiss him on the head. I'm going to miss him.

Whatever it is that Annie is doing in her kitchen, it's loud and annoying. She's banging pans together and slamming cabinets. Knowing she probably wants my attention, I choose to ignore it.

I open my purse and take out my bottle of ibuprofen. Just as I open the bottle, something shifts in me and I change my mind. I toss it back into my purse. I think I need to feel all of this.

I review everything that Harold confided in me and it hurts my heart. Did Bobby really leave her? Was she always this way? Harold said she changed after he died. I wonder if she was ever happy. She doesn't ever seem to be. I guess I can relate to that.

My life has consisted of work and avoiding people for the last few years. I've had zero social life up until

I started following around a little nasty old lady. Since then, I've had two men ask me out in the last week. Shit! I remember Adam is going to be at my house at seven. I need to talk to Annie and finish what I started. Enough is enough.

Trudging into her kitchen, I see she's kneading dough. She's pounding it and flipping it around as if she's mad at it.

"What did that bread do to you?" I ask.

"Say what you gotta say and let's get this over with."

"Fine." I cross my arms. "You've left ten reviews for products this week that I could find. Ten. Yet when I asked you if you'd written any you told me you'd only written one. You knew I needed at least three for this article. Why would you keep them from me?"

"You asked me if I wrote one for Scotch. I said no. I didn't say I wasn't writing others."

"Annie, please!"

"I was going to tell you, but I got busy."

"You reviewed a book? Did you read it?"

"No."

"Then why review it? Why would you say something nasty about someone you don't even know?"

"Who said it was nasty?" she says, turning to face me.

I sigh at her.

She faces her dough and pounds it again.

"You also left a review for salad tongs. Did that have anything to do with what happened at the dollar store?"

She shrugs. "Maybe."

"But they weren't even the same brand. You said they were made so cheaply they couldn't pick up a piece of floss much less a wilted lettuce leaf."

"Floss," she says with a snicker. "Butt floss."

"Seriously! Do you realize that other people read the reviews you write? Do you understand the people who make these products rely on the income to survive and feed their families? How do you think it makes an author feel when you say their book is shit and it hasn't even been released yet?"

"I never said it was shit. I said she should 'save' her money."

I lower my head and shake it slowly.

"I don't need to explain anything I do to you or anyone else. I have my reasons."

I stand and walk over to her. "Tell me then! Tell me why you take so much pleasure in causing other people pain."

"You knew I wrote that review for your sister's bakery before you came here, didn't you?" she asks as she flips the bread over and adds more flour.

I rub my forehead, my frustration growing. "You're changing the subject."

"I'm not dumb, Ms. Joslyn Walters, fact-checker. Whatchoo gettin' out of this article? Because I know ain't no one just want to know how an old lady writes reviews."

I pretend to study the floor so I don't have to look at her.

"I don't care what nobody thinks of me. I haven't cared in a long time. People talk. They say things. It's gonna happen. The world isn't fair, child. You all been brought up to think you deserve an award for showing up. Life is a battle ground and we all have to choose what side we want to be on."

"If you're going to comment on other people's things, why not say something positive? Why not make the world a better place instead of contributing to its demise?"

"You don't know nothin' about me."

"You're right, I don't think I do. Do you know what people call you? They call you Angry Annie. Yep, that's your nickname. Because that's all you are to everyone, just plain angry."

"Get out of my house!"

Gritting my teeth, I walk over to the couch, reach into my wallet, and pull out five crisp twenty-dollar bills. I quietly put them on her kitchen table, take one last look at her, and walk out her door.

Rhode's car is still in the driveway. As much as I'd like to go see him and spill my guts, I know Adam will be coming over soon. I need to find out what he knows. As I walk to my car, I want to toss my lunch. I *don't* want to lose Rhode. I *do* care about him. In some odd way, I actually care about Annie too. What's happened to me?

I decide after Adam leaves, I'll call Rhode and tell him everything. I have to write this article. What choice do I have? My reputation is on the line. If it gets published, he'll need to understand why I did what I did. He needs to hear it from me. Maybe someday, Annie can forgive me too.

At seven on the dot, there's a knock on my door. Begrudgingly I open it to Adam's smiling face. He's carrying a bottle of wine.

"Adam, this isn't a date."

"I'll take what I can get. I'm going to grow on you, Joss."

"Like fungus," I mumble.

"What was that?" he asks, leaning in.

"Nothing. Now what did you want to tell me?"

"Can we at least have a drink first?"

I nod and motion toward the kitchen. Opening a drawer, I hand him my cork screw.

"Nice place," he says, gazing around.

As I follow his line of sight, I realize the place does look pretty damn good. After I got home from my parents' house, I started cleaning. I wanted to think things through and surprisingly, cleaning and thinking worked well together. I don't know when I ever really cleaned anything before this week. Now my car is clean, my apartment is organized, and even my purse is tidy. It's amazing what a few days out of a routine can do you for you. Or maybe a few days with a neat freak.

He pops the cork and I hand him a glass.

"Do you have another?"

"I'm not drinking. Adam, please just tell me what you know."

He pours the wine and takes a sip, leaning on the counter. "You look different today. I like the waves in your hair."

"I got caught in the rain."

"It's not just that. There's something else that's changed. You look, I don't know. Like you're glow-ing."

Sex. It must be the mind-blowing sex I had today. Or maybe it's because my heart is changing. Maybe it's because I'm letting myself feel for the first time in my life.

"I'd like to be the one who makes your skin glow," he says, taking a step closer and lifting his hand to touch my face.

"Adam, no. I'm seeing someone. This isn't going to happen with us. We're friends and that's all." Phew. It feels good to get that off my chest. When did I start keeping things inside?

"Friendships change."

I swear if he doesn't stop making small talk he's going to have to arrest me for assaulting an officer. "You said you had news?"

"Right." He nods as he takes another drink. "I did a little research on Annie McClintonuck. As it turns out, it's not her legal name. Her real name is Annie Gibson. Sometime over the last thirty years she started using McClintonuck, but it's an alias. It's one of the reasons you couldn't find her. The only reason I was able to pull her up was because she filed a report against a neighbor of hers about ten years ago for playing their music too loud. I guess they finally had enough and moved out. They said she was a pain in the ass."

"Holy crap!" I rush over to my laptop and search Thea McClintonuck. Sure as shit, her name comes up with her address. I search for Bobby. I need to know the truth.

Someone knocks on my door. "Do you want me to get that?" Adam asks, motioning to the door.

"No. Leave it." I wave him off as they knock again. An article pops up about a train accident. Bobby McClintonuck was killed when he stepped in front of a train. I gasp.

"You again?"

I turn my head to see a bouquet of pink roses in someone's hand. I jump up from my seat.

"Is Joslyn here?"

I know that voice. It makes my heart flutter. I bite my nail. What do I do?

"Yes, she is."

"Excuse me. I didn't mean to interrupt."

"Well, you did. Again."

"Could you give these to her?" He hands the flowers to Adam and spins on his heel.

"Wait!" I shout.

He's halfway down the stairs when I reach him.

"Rhode, it's not what it looks like!"

"Really?" he questions. "Because it looks like I broke in on another date with Officer Not So Friendly."

"It's not a date. I swear," I say, reaching for his arm.

"And the other night wasn't a date either then?"

"No. Well, yes. Technically it was, but it was only because I had to."

"Did you have to sleep with me today too?"

I grit my teeth and place my hands on my hips. "That was an awful thing to say. You should know the answer to that. Today was amazing."

"Not amazing enough for you to accept a date with me. However, you seem to always have time for Adam. I guess the men in uniform always get the girl."

"Adam *doesn't* get the girl. He doesn't have me and he never will. The only reason he's here is because he had info on Annie."

"Annie!" He throws his hands in the air, waving the roses. "Why are you so obsessed with her? And what happened between you two? She wasn't herself tonight."

"You saw her?"

"How do you think I got your address? You know I care about the both of you. Tell me what's going on."

"I want to. I really do. But I'm afraid you won't understand."

"I wouldn't, huh? Does Adam understand?" has asks, motioning to the apartment. He's pissed. I can tell by the gleam in his eyes.

I shake my head. I'm saying all the wrong things.

"Annie told me something tonight about you and I didn't believe her. She said the article you were writing about her was all a lie. I told her you'd never lie. I said you'd never hurt someone for your own benefit. Please tell me she was wrong about you."

My chin dips down and my voice comes out in a whisper. "I didn't want to hurt anyone."

His free hand flies to the top of his head. "So it's true? You lied to me? You lied to Annie?"

"I didn't know you like I do now. I was going to tell you."

"Tell me what? That you were using me like you used Annie? For a story? Was the pathetic grass cutter going to get a shout out in this exposition? Were you going to tell the world how I fell for you and wanted to date you while you laughed with your real boyfriend behind my back?"

"Adam? Adam is just a friend. I swear!"

"Does Adam think he's just a friend? Because I think he believes he's a hell of a lot more."

I sigh.

"Maybe you lied to him too. Maybe you even lie to yourself." He steps away and turns back to face me. "Here, Annie asked me to give you this."

He pulls a flash drive from his pocket. "Do what you want with it. It doesn't matter anymore."

He starts to walk away.

"Rhode, please don't leave. Come inside. Let me explain."

"Should I join you and Adam? Do you need more information from me about Annie or is it Adam's turn to be your source?" he asks, pointing up the stairs. "No, thanks. I'll see you around, Joss. I don't like being used."

"Really? That's what you think about me? That's how you're going to be? Is that how quickly you give up? I thought you wanted to be with me."

"I did."

"But not anymore?"

He sighs and pushes his hands into his pockets.

I tug on his sleeve and move in closer to him. He seems to try to read me.

"Please give me a chance."

"Joss, you need any help?" Adam yells from the second floor.

Rhode nods to me. I don't like the way he's looking at me. It's like the light is gone. He smiles, but it doesn't touch his eyes. "Good night, Joss. Good luck with your article. I hope you get everything you wanted."

He jogs across the parking lot and hops into his car. I want to chase him, but I know it won't do me any good. The truth is, he's probably better off without me.

# CHAPTER Twenty-two

I **WAKE UP AT** 3:00 a.m. to the sound of a car alarm blaring outside. After I made Adam leave, I called Rhode. He didn't answer his phone and I didn't leave a message.

I wanted to tell him I'm crazy about him, but I couldn't bring myself to say it. Especially now that I know he'll never look at me the same way again. I really blew it.

I finished the bottle of wine Adam left, curled up on the couch, and cried myself to sleep. I can tell because my couch pillow has a big wet spot and my hair is matted to my head on one side.

Pushing up from the sofa, I hear something hit the ground. It's the flash drive Rhode gave me from Annie. I forgot all about it.

Curiosity pulls me out of my drowsy state and I sit down at my computer. I turn it over in my fingers a few times. How in the world did Annie make this? Her computer is so old, it probably still uses floppy disks. I guess maybe it wasn't as old as I thought. I'd like one day to go by where I'm not wrong about something.

Just one.

I plug it into the drive and watch the files download on my screen. I stop counting at thirty. They just keep coming. Every file starts with the word review followed by shoes, bird feeders, books, stores, underwear . . . the list is endless. Hussy lipstick catches my eye and I snicker. Rubbing my eyes, I shake my head in disbelief. I think she's given me every review she's ever written. The cursor finally ends with a file named Review – Joslyn.

Leaning back in my chair, nausea hits me hard. Did she review me?

I click on the file. Word opens. It's a letter.

*Dear Liar,*

*Yesterday when you left to find Stupid, I did some snooping of my own. I found your notebook on me as well as a release form you never had me sign. I mailed it to your office because, like I told you before, I don't care what you think about me. I don't care what anyone thinks.*

*But, I'm gonna tell you my story for my own piece of mind and because you paid me to. A deal is a deal.*

*My name is Annie Gibson, not McClintonuck. I liked that name better, so I took it. It was supposed to be mine anyway and a promise is a promise.*

*I've always considered myself a word connoisseur. I fancy words and the way they can be put together to bring emotion. For many years I was paid well to put those words in a certain order for a greeting card company. I believed every word I said, until one day I didn't.*

*Bobby was the love of my life and I was his. I did rock his world with my pooty, but he didn't die because of me. He died because of the world. Because the pressures of the world were too great to bear. I said he died because of his heart, but the truth was it was my heart that suffered.*

*The night he died, I let go of all my plans for the future. There would be no wedding, no home with a white picket fence, no children, and no grandchildren. There wouldn't be a happy ever after for me. I accepted my fate.*

*I wrote greeting cards for years after that. My niche became the sympathy cards. I could write a sappy note that could make war criminals cry. And then, I didn't want to anymore. I got over it.*

*It was all doom and gloom. It wasn't how I felt anymore. It wasn't me. So I started writing what I called my get real cards. I thought they were a hoot. Not everyone was sad when a loved one died. Sometimes it was a relief. Boss didn't like the card that said, "I heard of your momma's passing," on the front and "Sure took long enough," on the inside. But good Lord Almighty, I bet you that woulda sold like hot cakes!*

*He moved me to a happier place. Birthday celebrations. But he didn't like my ideas for those either. I wrote cards for birthdays that said, "You still alive? Why don't you drop dead already?" Boss said he thought I'd lost my mind. I had a feeling he was gonna let me go, so I quit. I didn't need to work. Bobby left me everything, including his sister, Thea. Plus, I ain't never spent a penny. People seem to like giving me money and food and shit. I don't stop them. I got no reason to.*

*But not writing no more, well, it hurt my heart. One day, the Lord sent me a sign. After I watched a waitress talk down to a homeless man, I felt I needed to say something about it. I about lost my ass. So I reviewed the place.*

*And you know what happened? People liked it. They responded to it. Some people thanked me. Some people yelled at the owner and demanded he change his staff. Some people even told me to mind my business. But it gave me something to do and someone to talk to.*

*After a while, I realized people responded to the bad more than the good. And when it would get lonely, I'd write a review, sit back, and wait to see what happened. Some people stopped believing what I said and that didn't really bother me. I liked the negative comments more than the good because it fueled my fire. I liked that my words made people speak up. I figured it was better to yell at me than not say anything at all. It gave me pleasure to know a bad review from me meant other people would want to know more and find out for themselves.*

*Now, don't get me wrong. Some of this stuff pissed me off to high heaven in a Jesus quilt. But mostly, I wrote what I thought would get people angry.*

*Angry Annie. Yep, that's me. I'm an old, angry woman. I hate the world and everything in it. I hate my stupid cat Stupid who refuses to leave me even when I tell him I wish I'd never laid eyes on him. I hate my greedy, old, sort of boss who lets me come in and stock shelves just so I have somewhere to go. I hate my lawn-*

*mowin' annoying neighbor who brings me some of the worst tasting food I've ever had and checks up on me every day even though I tell him he makes me physically ill. And I hate this blond hussy who showed up at my door actin' like she knew what made the sky blue and gave me a reason to get up in the morning.*

*You know why I wrote that review for your sister's bakery? It wasn't 'cause I wanted her to go away, even though she coulda picked a better color to paint the outside. It really is an eye sore. I wrote it 'cause I knew I'd get it some attention. So take that pill and shove it up your hooty tooty know-it-all ass.*

*Child, you got a lot to learn about life, about men, and about old people. Growing old doesn't harden your heart. We force ourselves to get harder on the outside 'cause we gotta protect the mush from seeping out. You should spend more time lookin' through other people's eyes and less time assuming you got the world figured out. Nothin' is ever the way it seems. You is dumber than Stupid and that's saying a lot 'cause we all know how many times he's hit his head walkin' into a wall.*

*There's a reason you didn't get reviews from me. And the only reason I'm telling you is 'cause I know I ain't ever gonna have to lay eyes on your ugly, twiggy, whiney ass ever again. I didn't give you my reviews because I knew the minute you got them, you'd be gone. And, well, when you flip over a crab, you see the softness under his shell. And sometimes we crabs have to take what we can get while we can get it.*

*So write your article about me. Tell the world I'm angry, 'cause I am. This life ain't always been good to me, but for some reason, I'm still kickin' through it.*

*Every once in a while I get me a bag of lemons and a chance to use them. I live for the lemons.*

*And for the sake of all things green, make sure you keep that boy busy. He's cut my grass twice this week and he needs to mow someone else's lawn for a change. He cuts grass when he's worried and after you left yesterday he cut mine again. You keep this up and I'm gonna have to get AstroTurf.*

*Good riddance,*
*Angry Annie*

I don't even realize I'm sobbing until I come to the end. How can one week with a complete stranger make you question your entire life, your goals, and everything you thought you wanted to be?

I stand and walk the room. Everything looks and feels different now. A week ago I was so certain I'd do anything to get ahead. I was so certain I had Annie pegged for a horrible person. But was she really ever that bad?

I think about the night I found her with the bottle of scotch. I remember Rhode telling me she meant the opposite of what she said. I remember her door being unlocked and a cup of coffee poured for me even though she claimed she never wanted to see me again. But she did want to see me. And as I look back, I wanted to see her too.

I turn off the lights and walk into my bedroom. There's a glow coming through the window from the street lamp and I sit on the bed and let it shine on my legs. I think about the bathroom at the dollar store and my foot stuck in the toilet bowl and I smile. She made me laugh, a lot.

How can I go back to work and write an article about what a horrible person she is when I'm not sure I think she was ever terrible to begin with? When right now, I feel like I'm the terrible one? When deep down inside I want to be more like her than I care to admit? How can I tell the world that this particular Internet troll is an awful human being when I'm a bigger liar than she ever was? Every troll has a tale and Annie's story isn't at all what I expected.

I close my eyes and I see Rhode's face. I remember how he looked at me when he realized I'd been keeping the truth hidden away along with my feelings for him. How can I walk away from him, walk away from a man who makes my heart pound in my chest just by entering a room? How could I lie to the only guy who's ever made me want more?

Pushing up from the bed, I run my fingers through my hair. I can't. I can't do this. I'm not the same girl I was a week ago and I'll never be the same. Something has to give and this time it's going to be me.

# CHAPTER Twenty-three

I YAWN AS I sit outside Darla's office. A week ago I would have been a nervous wreck about presenting my article to her, but today I'm calm, cool, and collected.

I've been waiting for her since 6:00 a.m. It's almost eight and I'm going to have to come back later if I can't get in to see her. This meeting is taking forever. But coming back later doesn't bother me because I know one way or another I'm going to get her to read this article and my proposal. It's damn good if I do say so myself. It could change everything for all of us, assuming I can get Annie to cooperate and Darla to buy into it. Annie is step two. I need to get in the door with Darla before I can sit at the desk with Annie.

The doors open suddenly and unhappy, flustered people race out of her office like ants on a hill sprayed with bug killer. I imagine myself as an ant trying to carry Annie on my back. I must be more tired than I realize. Apparently not sleeping in twenty-four hours will do that to a person.

"Back already?" She sighs as she notices me while

closing her door. "I suppose my week of quiet is over. If I tell you I'm busy, will you go away or are you going to sit out there all day until I listen?"

"Good morning," I say with a smile as I step into her office and place my article on her desk.

She sits down, lowers her glasses to the tip of her nose, and sighs. She picks up the papers and skims through the top page. "This isn't what we discussed."

"No, it's not. It's even better."

"Ms. Walters, what makes you think I have any interest in this sort of thing?" She drops my papers into her garbage can and shakes her head. "Good day."

"Hold on," I announce. "I know it's not the article I promised you, but you didn't even read it." I bend down and lift it out of the trash can, smoothing it out and placing it back on her desk.

"Yes, I had an idea, but the truth is the facts didn't add up the way I'd expected. Isn't it my journalistic responsibility to report the truth? Are there Internet trolls out there who write nasty reviews to hurt people? Absolutely, but this woman . . . she's not like them. She's mean and horrible, stubborn and crazy, but she also has a heart. She cares in her own way and she tells the truth whether people want to hear it or not. Sometimes we need the truth more than we realize."

I swallow hard when Darla focuses on her computer and makes a few clicks.

"One of the reasons I took this job was because I heard you managed the magazine. You have always been my idol. Until today."

Darla's eyes meet mine.

"Today I realized that a nasty, little old woman who's had a rough lonely life but fights her way through it is my idol. Because when it comes down to it, she cares. If you would take the time to look around this office, you'd see that every one of us has a story inside that makes for good cover. I'm telling you right now that I believe with my whole heart and soul, *The Gaggle's* sales would skyrocket if you'd just hear me out. If you'd take a chance."

"Are you finished?"

I meet her gaze with more confidence than I had before because at this moment I know she's not that different from me. She's just another human being and I'm not beneath her. "Yes, I'm finished. I've spent the last week being called every horrible name in the book. I've been stuck in a toilet bowl, lost a week of vacation, used my grocery money for a story, and met a man who rocked my world. This week changed my life and it changed me. You won't hear from me for three months as promised, but I also promise you this. I promise that in three months I'm going to hand you that article again. And I'll do it every day after that until I know you read my proposal and gave it the consideration it deserves. Thank you, Darla. Have a wonderful three months. I'll see you the very next day."

I leave her office with my head held high. I might have crossed a line and maybe I'll get fired for it, but in my heart, I know it was worth it. What good are lemons if you can't squeeze them in your own eyes and see things differently?

I feel in my gut that I did the right thing. A story is only as good as the heart behind it. I'm rewriting *my* story too. It needs a brand-new beginning and preferably, a happily ever after with a certain landscaper.

Sitting in the parking lot of Tyke's Tavern, I glance into the mirror for the hundredth time with the intention of fixing my hair and makeup. But every time I look in the mirror, I do a double take because I almost don't recognize myself.

I feel so different now and as I sit here, about to pour out my heart for the first time in my life, I worry he won't see things the way I do. I worry he won't let me explain. I usually don't overthink things, I just act. But this time I've planned out every scenario in my head. I'm more nervous about this than I've been about anything else in my life. Most likely because this involves my heart and up until a few days ago, I didn't believe I had one.

My cell phone lights up with a text and I drop it out of excitement. Turning it over, I say to no one, "Please let this work."

I read her text out loud. "He's on his way. Good luck, sissy. You've got this."

I swallow hard and close my eyes. He's coming. I glance over at the flower pot I put together for him and wonder if he'll understand.

Time passes slowly. I watch the door like the closet stalker that I am and my heart leaps when I see him, clad in tight-fitting jeans, a button-down flannel shirt, and a backward baseball cap. It's only been two days since I saw him last, but it feels like a lifetime.

As I walk into the bar carrying my gift, I offer a

silent prayer. Jorgie had to lie and tell him she wanted to meet about having some greenery added around the bakery. Hopefully, he's not upset that he gets me instead.

He's leaning on the bar with his lips pressed to the tip of a bottle of beer when I sneak in and position myself by the back wall. I stand directly behind him but at a distance, hoping and praying he'll gaze into the mirror. I need a redo.

An eternity passes as he finishes his beer. During that time, he gazes at his phone, at the door, and at his beer, but never looks in the mirror. Of course not. He's too modest to think anything about himself. Maybe this was a dumb idea.

A slender brunette with a plunging neckline leans on his back as she places a drink order and I suddenly have the urge to start a cat fight.

He smiles, shakes his head, and says something to her. She gets her drink, nods, and walks away. That's right, skankoliscous. He's mine. Walk away. Walk away!

Then it happens. His eyes meet mine in the reflection behind the bar. I smile at him the way he smiled at me the first time I saw him, but instead of being happy to see me, he tosses some cash on the bar and walks out the door.

I chase after him. "Rhode Bennett! Stop right there!"

He keeps walking and I can barely catch up to him. This plant is heavier than it looks. I shouldn't have watered it.

He's almost to his car when I catch my heel on a

crack and fall to the ground. The planter breaks into pieces when it hits the ground, creating a crashing echo across the parking lot.

My ego is bruised along with my knee as a trickle of blood slides down my shin.

Strong arms reach out for me. "Are you all right?"

With tears in my eyes I look up to Adam's face. My heart drops.

"I'm fine. Go away." Pushing his hands away forcefully, I decide I'd rather stay on the ground than have him touch me.

"Whoa," he says taking a step back. "I was just trying to help."

"Haven't you done enough?"

"What did I do?"

I sigh. "Do you remember that guy from the restaurant who came to my house last night? Well, I love him. I want him. And you keep showing up at the wrong time and the wrong place."

His eyes are soft. "You love him?"

"Yes, I do. And I need you to hear it loud and clear. Whether he wants me or not, I'm going to fight for him like I fight for everything else in my life."

He tries to help me stand and I push him away again. "I'm fine. Just go. Please. I'm sorry, Adam. You're a really great guy, just not the one for me."

He bends down to me. "I kind of figured that. But you can't blame a guy for trying can you?"

I smile because I feel awful for so many reasons. This wasn't a scenario I'd imagined.

"I think I've got this now." His voice causes my heart to pound in my chest.

Adam holds out his hand to Rhode and he shakes it. Adam smiles, nods to us, and jogs into the bar. I watch him only because I'm afraid to look at Rhode.

"What are you doing, Joss?" he asks as he crouches down next to me.

I shrug because I'm honestly not sure.

He pulls a handkerchief from his pocket and presses it to my knee. "Can you stand?"

I nod and he helps me up.

"You shouldn't run in heels."

"You shouldn't make me run," I reply curtly.

He snickers. "So Adam is done?" he asks, stuffing his hands into his pockets.

Fear grips me and I swallow hard as I brush off my skirt. "Did you hear us?"

"Did you think I'd really leave you alone in a bar parking lot, let alone on the ground?"

I shake my head.

"Did you mean it?"

Gazing into his eyes I reply confidently, "Every single word."

He tries to hold back a smile, but I don't know why. "What's all this?" he asks, pointing to the dirt.

"Forget it. It was a dumb idea. The whole thing was dumb. Annie was right about me. I don't have a clue." I dab my knee. The bleeding seems to have stopped, but I definitely left a mark on my knee to match the one on my ego.

"Snapdragons?" he asks as he lifts the broken pot and reclaims the flowers.

I nod.

"Now I need to know."

I shrug. I don't want to talk anymore because my plan went to shit. I didn't expect him to run.

"Tell me."

I take a deep breath and stare at the ground because looking into his eyes just reminds me he doesn't want anything to do with me anymore.

"They're pretty on the outside, but if you squeeze them they look like they could hurt you. Like a dragon. But the truth is, they don't want to hurt anyone even if they sometimes do it anyway. Maybe they're scared and they scare you away when you touch them. But deep down, they want to be as pretty on the inside as they are on the outside. It takes someone who wants to water them and care about them for them to ever grow into the flower they're supposed to be."

His head bends down and he squints up at me shyly with a slight smile. "Did they tell you all that?"

"Yeah. I'm a plant whisperer on the side."

He shakes his head at my sarcasm.

"I ruined them, though. I dropped them and now they're worthless."

"It's nothing that can't be fixed," he replies, gazing into my eyes. "Nothing is ever really broken."

I cover my face with my hands. He used my grandfather's words and it breaks my heart.

"I don't know what I'm doing!" I shout through my hands. "This isn't me. I don't run after hot guys in parking lots and bring them flowers and make up dumb analogies because I'm afraid to say what I really feel! I usually avoid feeling altogether."

"You think I'm hot?" he asks with a wink.

"So, so hot."

His smile fades as he gazes into my eyes. There's so much more I need to say.

"I'm sorry, Rhode. I never wanted to lie to you. I didn't think it was a big deal at first because I thought Annie deserved everything I was going to give to her."

"And now?"

"Now, I miss her and I miss you. I really miss you. And I want you to look at me like you did up until the other day. I want to be the best me I can be because of you. I grew up with a sister who was selfless to my selfish. She was the sweet to my salty and I thought that was the way it was supposed to be. But damn if you don't make me want to be whipped cream with a cherry on top."

"You sound like Annie."

"Is that a bad thing?" I ask, reaching out for him, then pulling away.

"Why did you do that?"

"I don't know why I did it. I thought I was willing to sacrifice everything for the sake of a by-line. But really, I'll sacrifice everything for the sake of you."

He smiles. "I meant, why did pull away and not touch me?"

"You want me to touch you?" I ask shyly.

"You should have touched a lot more."

I smirk as he uses my words against me. "Do you think you could give me another chance?"

"What did you have in mind?"

"Can I buy you a drink? Maybe date you for a while? Is that possible? Will you have me?" I feel insecure for the first time in my life. But sometimes you have to be weak before you can be strong.

"Your roots run deep, Joss. They were set inside me from the second I saw you."

"Is that a yes? The plant stuff is really over my head."

He drops the flowers to the ground and pulls me tightly against his chest. "It's a yes to all of it and just so you know, I love you too. You're exactly what I never knew I needed."

Placing my hands in his hair, I press my lips against his. My heart feels full for the first time in my life because I know with him by my side, my grass will always be green and I can handle all the lemons life throws at me.

# CHAPTER Twenty-four

RHODE KISSES ME ON the cheek. "Come back alive, please."

"If I'm not back in an hour, send reinforcements."

"You've got this."

I nod as I walk out his front door and count my steps to Annie's front porch.

There's a new sign on the front door. I place my new pot of snapdragons next to her door and read the improvements with a smile.

"No hussies. No liars. No solicitors. I don't like cookies. I've found my Lord and Savior. I already have an alarm. I don't need you to cut my grass. I don't like raffle tickets or children. I don't care if you're putting yourself through school, I'm not buying. I don't donate anything to anyone. Beware the dog, he bites. I don't need any new friends. I don't care if you just moved in. I know who I'm voting for and don't want to hear your opinions. Don't ring the bell. Don't knock. Don't stand on my porch. Don't tell me I'm famous. I already know. Stay away. I'll never like you. They call me Angry Annie for a reason."

Shaking my head, I pull a pen out of my purse and add a line to the bottom. "Don't believe anything I say. I don't mean it."

I smile at my creation. It's much better. As I'm about to knock, my phone rings. It says Seamore Publications, where I work, but if it were Claus, his name should come up on caller ID. I don't know who else would call.

"Hello?"

"Joslyn Walters, I read your proposal. Make it happen. You got what you wanted. Bring her in."

My eyes bulge wide and I hop up and down excitedly. "You won't regret this, Darla!"

"Oh, believe me, I already do." She laughs. "I'm proud of you. Good work."

Holy hell. Life is falling into place. I've convinced Rhode and Darla, but they were like petting puppies compared to the beast I'm about to face.

As I stand in front of Annie's house I realize shit just got even more real. I got the man, now I need the woman. Breaking Rhode was one thing, Annie is another story altogether.

I ring her bell and push my face up to the bars on the window to see inside. Rhode told me he saw her get her paper this morning, so I know she's in there.

She's mumbling something as she stomps to the door. I smile at her through the bars and she stops cold in her tracks, turns around, and walks back toward the kitchen.

I ring the bell again and again. Then I ring it to the tune of "Who let the dogs out." She still doesn't answer. “I have all day, Angry Annie!” I shout.

Her door flies open. “Can’t you read?” she shouts. “Go away. I don’t want none of what you sellin’.”

“Did you miss me?” I ask with a smile. “I brought you something!”

She makes that clicking sound with her teeth and scowls at me. “Unless it’s cold hard cash, I don’t give a rat’s ass.”

I lift the pot from the ground. “It’s better. It’s a flower.”

She tries to close the door on me, but I put my foot inside.

“Child, if you want to keep that scrawny foot, I suggest you get it the fuck out my door or I’m going to slam it till it closes, foot or no foot.”

“Can we talk? Please?”

“I ain’t got nothin’ to say to you.”

“I know you don’t. I have something to say to you.”

“I don’t care what you gotta say. I never did and I never will.”

I sigh. “When I first met Rhode he told me you meant the opposite of everything. I didn’t believe him back then, but I do now.”

“Oh, yeah. Well, then I think you is sweet as pie and I want you to never ever go away.”

I smile. “You’re not going to get me to leave until you hear me out. You had a chance to tell me your side, now can I have a chance to say mine?”

“No.”

“I’ll ring your doorbell all day long.”

“I’ll call the cops.”

“I have a friend there.”

"You ain't got no friends. Ain't nobody like your sorry lyin' ass."

"You like me. I know you do. And I like you too, Annie. Now please let me in before my foot falls asleep."

She breathes deeply and stares me down. It's another competition. A week or two ago, I thought I was the queen of them. Right now, I don't care about winning anything but her friendship. I smile at her and she shakes her head.

"Oh, for the sake of fuck, you got one minute."

Stepping into her foyer feels like coming home. It's only been a little over a week since I saw her last, but I feel like I've been away my whole life.

She crosses her arms and looks at her watch. "Tick tock, Joss."

"I'm sorry. I'm sorry that I looked at a toad and didn't see the royalty living inside of it."

"Child, you still make no sense. Say what you gotta say and get it over with. I ain't got time to analyze your bullshit."

"You're right. The honest truth, Annie, is that I was wrong about you. I thought I knew who you were and what kind of a person you were. Spending time with you made me see there are layers and layers to you."

"I ain't no onion. You got twenty seconds."

"Annie, please forgive me. I didn't write the article. I mean, I wrote an article but not one you'd expect."

"Ten seconds."

I quickly blurt out, "How does a weekly paycheck sound?"

Her mouth shifts in circles as she stares at me and

makes the clicking noise I now miss. "I'm listenin'."

"If there's one thing I can count on with you, it's that you won't sugarcoat the truth. We need more of that in this world. Like you said before, everywhere we go, people want to sell a ship we can't sail with a promise that won't float. Sometimes we need the truth, no matter how much it hurts. This is what I told my boss. And guess what? She wants it. She wants you."

"Whatchoo talkin' about? You done lost your mind."

She waves at me as she walks toward the kitchen. I follow her.

"*The Gaggle* wants to offer you a job. You would have a monthly column called Angry Annie where people write in with their problems and you tell them what to do."

She sits down at her table and takes a sip of coffee. "That's dumb."

"No, it's not. It's brilliant. You have so much to share, Annie. Do you have any idea how many people follow your reviews?"

She shakes her head.

"Seventeen thousand, four hundred and twenty-two people. Mostly between the ages of fourteen and thirty. Mostly women. But we could make you a household name. Move over, Dear Abby! Here comes Angry Annie!"

"I don't wanna be no household name!" she shouts, pushing off from her chair. "You need to go. I got stuff to do."

Furrowing my brows, I struggle with the words to reach her. "We'd be working together," I say with a smile.

"Oh, that makes a difference," she says, rolling her eyes. "Why didn't you say so to begin with? Now I can say beyond a shadow of a doubt, not in a million trillion years do I ever want to have to see you or talk to you every single day, ever again."

"I don't believe you," I say, folding my arms. "You said you didn't give me the reviews because you didn't want me to go away."

"I lied. I'm a liar too. Takes one to know one." Annie stomps to her front door and pulls it open. "Now get out. I got somewhere I have to be."

I gaze down at the snapdragons I'm still holding in my hands and place them down on her table.

I somberly walk to her door and stop just before I reach it. I lift a finger in the air. "I need to say one last thing."

"Oh, Lawd Jesus. Ain't that a surprise."

"You and I aren't that different. We may seem like total opposites but sometimes opposites make the best pairs. You taught me a lot about myself, Annie. You made me open my heart and my eyes. Even if you never speak to me again, you'll always be a part of me. No one can take that away. Not even you."

"Take your weed with you. I don't want that."

Gazing at the flower for a moment, I hope it works its magic on Annie like it did on Rhode. "It's not a weed. It's a snapdragon. I'm not taking it with me. I'm leaving it for you to remind you of me. It's tall and skinny, but it grows better in bunches. It only looks bad when you squeeze it too hard. I squeezed too hard."

"Guess now you don't get your big break," she

says with a cocky smile.

I shrug. "I didn't know they liked my idea until a few minutes ago. I was already on my way here to talk to you. It doesn't mean that much to me anymore. Someday, I'll do something great. I have a lot to learn."

As I walk down the steps, I feel her eyes boring into my back.

"How much?"

"How much what?" I ask, turning to face her.

"How much this job pay? I ain't workin' for peanuts."

Annie doesn't have to say she forgives me for me to know what's in her heart. She may be angry on the outside, but that inside is gold. I see it and someday maybe she will too.

# CHAPTER Twenty-five

*Three months later*

LIFTING THE BLINDS, *I* try my best to peek out through the crack at Annie's house. "Are you sure that's what she said?" I ask, turning briefly to look at Rhode.

"I'm sure."

"Tell me again. Word for word."

He huffs. "She said she didn't want dinner tonight. She said she had plans."

"That's not word for word."

He sighs. "Okay, fine. I believe it was, 'I don't need your stinkin' tacos. I'm getting' my own.'"

"With who?" I ask protectively. "Who's getting her tacos? Do we know this person? What if it's someone who read her column and wants to take advantage of her?"

Rhode laughs. "I think Annie can handle herself, Joss." He pops a piece of popcorn into his mouth and I bite at my nails.

"Come on, babe. It's date night. Annie is going to be just fine. I know you two are all besties now, but if she needed something she'd call. Now, are you going to stare out the window all night or are you going to sit next to me and watch a romantic movie that's sure to make you want to have sex?"

Twisting my mouth, I place my finger against my cheek like I'm thinking. "Such a tough call. Who do I get to have sex with?"

He crosses his legs at the ankles and leans back against his couch. "He's a professional landscaper. Very skilled. He heard your grass needed to be mowed and he's even willing to plant his flowers in you for free."

"Plant his flowers?" I laugh.

"I have an overabundance of seeds. They're multiplying by the minute."

"Oh, really?" I ask, sitting next to him on the sofa.

He pushes a hair away from my face and stares into my eyes. "Do you know how beautiful you are?"

I sigh. "Let's skip the movie and go garden now."

"No, no, no. I promised you a date. Since you insisted we stay in and spy on Annie, I'm going to insist we watch at least half of this movie."

"Are you sure you're the guy and not me? I'd think you'd rather get me naked than stare at a TV screen."

His eyes darken as he adjusts the bulge in his pants. "I want you. You know that. But I also love you and I want to show you in every way possible."

"Where have you been all my life?" I ask as I take off his baseball cap and place it on my head.

"Waiting for you."

A car door slams outside and I jump up from my seat and rush over to the blinds. "Shit! I can't see anything. Someone is parked in front of her house."

"Who?" he questions.

"I can't tell, but I see a shadow walking up the path."

"Maybe we should go outside and make sure everything is okay."

Tilting my head to the side, I can't help but raise my eyebrows. "What happened to Annie can take care of herself?"

"She can," he says, lifting to his feet. "I just want you to feel better about it. Anything for you."

"Uh-huh," I say knowingly. There's only one person I know who loves Annie as much as I do and I'm looking at him. We've turned into protective parents.

He grabs my ass as he walks past me and I bite my lip. It may have taken me a lifetime to fall in love, but I'm certain I never understood what it was all about until he came along. He makes me laugh, cry, and feel all the things. I think the reason I never felt this way before I met him was because I hadn't met him yet.

"Are you coming?" he half whispers, half shouts as he stands in the open door.

I bolt from the window and we tiptoe across his lawn. We carefully scoot to the side of the house, staying as low as possible so she doesn't see us. There's a light on inside, but I can't see anyone.

"Let's try the other side," he suggests.

I hold on to his arm as we sneak around Annie's house in the dark.

"This is really turning me on," I whisper. Maybe we should do it outside tonight.

"Shh . . ." he whispers. "Do you hear that?"

Focusing on the sound, we stare at the ground. We both turn to each other in fear when we hear Annie scream out in pain.

"Oh my God, Rhode!" I shout in fear as his expression mimics mine.

We rush to her front door. It's locked.

"Your key!" I shout as my hands fly to my head and I grip my face. "Get away from her!" I scream into the air, hoping whoever is hurting her can hear me.

Rhode pats his chest then his legs before he produces his keychain. He fumbles with them before he's able to find the key and turn it in the lock.

"We're coming, Annie!" I shout as he opens the door.

We run through the house to her bedroom and slam the door open.

The first thing I see is a hairy gray ass in the air. Annie is under him and she's yelling, "Ooh, yeah, put that joystick in my donut! Get it in there good!"

"Holy shit!" I scream, turning away.

"What the ever lovin' fuck?" Annie shouts as the man climbs off her. "Whatchoo doin' in here?"

Rhode and I quickly close the door behind us and step into the hall. We stare at each other, faces pale like we saw a ghost. A ghostly ass.

Her door opens and she hoofs out the door, angry as can be, tying her robe. "What in the hell you doin' here?" she shouts, closing the door behind her.

"I'm so sorry, Annie!" I whisper, wringing my hands in embarrassment.

Rhode takes his baseball cap off my head and pulls it down over his eyes. "We thought you were in trouble."

"I was in trouble. I was 'bout to cum!"

"Oh, hell," Rhode says, placing his fingers in his ears.

My mouth hangs open in shock. After a few seconds, Annie thrusts her pelvis into the air and I start to laugh.

"No, no, no!" Rhode says. "I can't stop seeing it. It's there. I'm never going to be able to unsee it!"

"It'll be okay, babe!" I say with a small snicker. "It's just a part of life!"

Rhode leans on the wall and pulls his cap down to his mouth. "If I could crawl into the wall right now, I'd do it."

"You gonna be dreamin' of my boobs for the rest of your life," she says, patting him on the shoulder.

"Who is he?" I ask excitedly.

"I ain't talkin' about this now. He waitin'!"

"Oh, right!" I say, cringing.

"Is that my cupcake I hear?"

Turning to the familiar sound, I whimper when my half naked grandfather steps out of Annie's bedroom.

"Hey there, Joss boss, bo boss—"

I lift my hand in the air and turn my face away. "Oh, hell no!"

Rhode laughs, pats me on the arm, and says, "It'll be okay, babe. It's just a part of life."

I punch him in the arm and he laughs harder.

"I didn't know I'd be seeing you tonight!" Wilbur says happily.

I can't form any words.

"I don't think she expected to see you tonight either," Annie says with a laugh. "I don't think she expected to see *any* of you."

I cover my face with my hands.

"So, um, Joss and I are going to go now," Rhode begins as he tugs on my arm, pulling me toward the door.

I leave my hands over my eyes as he leads me. "Bye, Grandpa."

"Bye bye, baby cakes. See you at dinner next week."

"Hold on a second, Willy," Annie says. "I'll be right back."

She follows me to the front step. "You okay with this?"

I swallow hard and peek at her through my fingers. "Are you happy?"

"You know, I think I might be."

My hands fall to my sides. "Then I'm more than okay. I'm happy with you."

A loud thump causes us both to turn as Stupid walks into a wall, shakes it out, and tries again, getting it right.

"I'll tell you, it was in front of my eyes the whole time."

"What was?" I question.

"Sometimes we all walk into walls, but we shake it off and try again until we get it right. That's what life is all about."

I nod. "You're absolutely right, Annie."

Life is a series of lessons. There's always something you can learn. People come and go from our lives with purpose. It's not random. And sometimes, when you least expect it, those passers-by turn into friends. If you're really lucky, those friends become family. I'm one of the lucky ones.

Lemons only suck if you let them. If you look hard enough, they might even be gold in disguise.

# THE END

# ACKNOWLEDGEMENTS

This book took me by surprise. One day, I was feeling kind of angry at the world and the next thing I knew, I'd made up a character named Annie. I love Annie with all my heart. She allowed me to vent through my story and clean out some wounds. Thanks Annie.

I couldn't have completed this book without the help and support of my friends, my family, and my friends who are my family. So to everyone here and everyone I might have missed, thank you!

To my boys, Tyler and Ryan. You'll always be first because you are my heart and soul. This year has been tough for us and I couldn't have made it through without you. I love you.

To my bestie, Kim Hurschik. Thanks for forcing me to go to the gym when I don't want to. Thanks for letting me tell you all my deepest, darkest secrets and fears and for never judging me. Thank you for threatening to beat up people who make me cry, even though I'd never let you actually do it. Thank you for 3:00 daily phone calls, sharing my hopes and dreams, listening to my ideas, telling me I can do it when I don't think I can, and for always encouraging me to be the best me that I can be. I love you, sister.

To Dorrie Cortesi. There will never be enough coffee dates, walks, texts, or phone calls for us, but we will always be friends no matter what life throws our way. Thank you for checking up on me and making me feel like I have a family on days I feel alone. Your support means more to me then you will ever know. Love you girl.

To Misty Marcum. Thank you for texts, FB messages, and phone calls to let me vent and make me smile. Thank you for helping me run my reader group and for always telling me when I should be doing more than I am. I think you're amazing and I want to be you when I grow up, even though I'm older than you. I flove you.

To Jennifer Mock. Thank you for your never ending belief in me. Your strength and bravery makes me want to be a better person. You always say you look up to me, but the truth is, it's me looking up to you. I don't know what I'd do without you and I love you to the moon and back.

To Hazel James. Woman… you rock. Thank you for being the calm to my crazy and for pretending I'm still cool when I act like an idiot. Thank you for your amazing feedback and for encouraging me to keep pushing through life's storms. I admire the shit out of you and I feel blessed to have you in my life. Love you tons.

To Brenna Leigh. It's funny how you can meet someone and feel as if you've known them your whole life. Thank you for always supporting me even when I don't deserve it. Thank you for reading all my words and being patient when I forget to send you books. More importantly, thank you for being an amazing proof-reader, and an even better friend. I expect holiday invitations now that I've invited myself into your family. Just kidding… or am I? I <3 U so freaking much.

To Andee Michelle. We may not get to talk as often as we like, but every time we do, it's like no time has passed. That's when you know you have a real friend. You are a rock for me and always have been. You've seen me through some really rough days and I love you like a sister. Thank you for reading for me and always being there. When you're ready, I'll eat your words for breakfast, lunch and dinner.

To The Twisted Chick-Lits. What a lucky girl I am to have you in my life. Thank you all for reading my stories, replying to my silly games, and always making me feel like I have a gang of people standing behind me with my back. I love each and every one of you and I'm grateful to call you my friends.

To Murphy Rae at Indie Solutions by Murphy Rae. Thank you for reading my mind and giving me the perfect cover. We've been working together for four years now, and each time, you seem to get me a little more. I'm glad I can still surprise you. Thank you for being patient with me and my life. You're a great friend and I feel lucky to know you.

To Alyssa Garcia at Uplifting Designs. Thank you for taking me in and always responding to my confused messages! I can't wait to see what you come up with. <3.

To all my readers. Thank you for your support, your friendship, and your love. I wouldn't be who I am without you and I will never forget that. Thank you for believing in me and reading my words. You're the reason I keep doing what I do.

# ABOUT THE AUTHOR

Dawn L. Chiletz resides in Illinois with her two boys and three dogs. Her love of reading began at a young age and continued into adulthood. Armed with a dream from the night before, she sat down at her laptop in the summer of 2014 and started the words to her first book, *The Contest.* She's been writing ever since. When she's not binge reading or writing you can most likely find her on social media avoiding laundry.

To find out more information, including her upcoming signings, please visit her website at
www.dawnlchiletz.com

Follow her on her Facebook author page:
www.Facebook.com/dawnlchiletz

Join her Facebook reader group:
Dawn's Twisted Chick-Lits
www.Facebook.com/groups/1740692116171170

Instagram:
www.Instagram.com/dawnlchiletz

Twitter:
www.twitter.com/dawnlchiletz

# OTHER TITLES BY DAWN L. CHILETZ

The Contest series:
*The Contest*
*Waiting to Lose*

Reality TV Novels:
*The Fabulist*
*The Praetorian*

Standalone Novels:
*Enough*
*Can't You See*
*Confessions of a Carpool Captive*